Purple Haze

George Hudson

Savant Books
Honolulu, HI, USA
2013

Published in the USA by Savant Books and Publications
2630 Kapiolani Blvd #1601
Honolulu, HI 96826
http://www.savantbooksandpublications.com

Printed in the USA

Edited by Sabrina Favors
Cover by Daniel S. Janik
Author photo by Gail Hudson

13 digit ISBN: 9780988664050
10-digit ISBN: 0988664054

Dedication

I dedicate this novel to Gail... my rock.

Acknowledgements

Thanks to Gloria Yeatman and Leonard Timm in Costa Rica for the initial proofing. Also, thanks to my brother, Joe, a lifetime employee of the TVA, and to the rest of my brothers and sisters, who encouraged me along the way. A special thanks to my editor, Sabrina Favors, for her patience with me on this, my first novel. I hope that there will be many more to follow.

Purple Haze

Chapter 1
Watts Bar Lake, Spring City, Tennessee
June 30, 1970

It was a miserable night for fishing. David Owenby and his long-time fishing buddy, Al Wilcox, had been coming out to this spot to fish for the past twenty years—ever since this lake had been open to the public. They had pooled their money together and bought a tract of land on Watts Bar Lake in Eastern Tennessee and had brought their families down every summer from Ohio to camp and fish.

The lake had been built in the 1940s as part of the New Deal project known as the Tennessee Valley Authority, "TVA." It provided low-cost power from the hydroelectric turbines generated by the dam along with recreational activities, including fishing, for the people of the Tennessee Valley and surrounding states.

This night had become a ritual for David and Al. Just the two of them, smoking cigars, drinking beer, eating snacks all night and fishing in their sixteen-foot aluminum boat. The day had begun bright and cheerful with a hot June sun shining incessantly. They had spent most of the day fishing from the bank with their two young sons, Josh, 12, and John, 11. It was great for the four of them to just sit on the bank and fish for bluegill, catching them almost as fast as they cast their lines. The boys had learned to bait their own hooks with worms, so it wasn't as much aggravation for the dads as it used to be. They had fished for about five hours off the bank, and then spent the better part of an hour cleaning fish for their supper. Afterwards, their wives pan-fried them, and they had a good meal before they set out for their night-fishing expedition.

They had arrived at their usual spot before dark, set out their lanterns, and put their minnow buckets, full of fresh shiners, in the water, before sitting back to enjoy a good cigar and a few tall tales before the fishing began in earnest about two hours after dark. Unfortunately, the weather was not cooperating with them tonight. The wind was blowing, creating an unsettling chop on the surface of the lake, made them feel uncomfortable. Though they had dropped small anchors from either end of the boat, the chop and resulting current made it difficult for them in the boat. It was imperative, with this style of fishing, to stay still so that the light would attract the bugs, which would land on the water and attract the minnows, which would in turn attract the fish. When things worked right, minnows would begin to appear and the serious fishing could start.

This evening, dark, cumulus clouds had begun to gather in the west before they even left the campsite. Both David and Al had felt that the clouds would simply blow by and that the night would be calm. But here they were, in the middle of an increasingly wicked lake and the wind was not only keeping the bugs away, but making them feel miserable.

"We've been out here for three hours now," complained David, "and I have not seen a single bug, let alone a minnow."

"Let's give it a little longer," said Al, trying not to sound as dejected as David. "Here, have a cup of coffee." He poured David a cup of hot, black coffee from his thermos and handed it to him.

David set the coffee to one side. "I think I'll try to go deep and see if I can catch a catfish on the bottom. We've always been able to catch them, and I did bring a bunch of night crawlers that the boys dug up this morning in the woods."

He reeled up his line and hooked on a wiggling night crawler and added extra weight to his line to take it quickly to the bottom. He eased his baited hook over the side of the boat and released the line so it quickly sank to the bottom. "Must be about fifty feet deep here," said David, as the line finally stopped unwinding. "That's about two-thirds of my reel out."

As the boat moved slowly with the current, it dragged the line along the bottom, and the movement created a bumping of the rod as the tip bobbed up and down. The two fishermen had both learned over the years to use heavy tackle for this style of fishing and the reels were loaded with twenty-pound test line on heavy, deep-sea-style rods.

While David was sipping on his coffee, he held the rod in his other hand waiting for a telltale bump or pull on his line. Al sat patiently in the front of the boat with his feet propped up on the stern, dozing, his cup of coffee on the seat beside him. Suddenly, Al was awakened as David's feet kicked excitedly against the bottom of the boat in response to a sharp tug on his line. He sat up erect and began hurriedly reeling in line.

"I think I've got a big catfish on here! Get ready with the dip net in case we need it," ordered David.

He continued to reel as hard as he could, and the tip of the fishing rod was bent almost to the water, but David could not feel movement on his line, just dead weight as he continued to reel his catch to the surface. Al moved to the back of the boat with the dip net to assist in the catch, spilling what was left of his coffee. As the hook neared the surface, Al lowered the net into the water near the line and prepared to land the monster, whatever it was.

"I don't think it's a fish," said David. "It doesn't seem to be moving any. Feels like a stick or something."

David suddenly stopped reeling and his eyes widened.

"What the hell is that?"

David lifted his line and a skull emerged from the water as Al put the dip net under it and brought it into the boat.

"Well, I'll be damned," said Al. He lifted up the skull and began to look at it closely. The hook had lodged into the lower part of the skull, and the eye sockets of the skull appeared to be looking right at the two fishermen as they moved it close to the lantern to look at it.

"What do we do with it?" asked David.

"What the hell do you think? We take it to the authorities. If there's a skull down there, there has to be a body to go with it."

"I can't think of a better ending to this miserable night than this," said David. He held the net over his head and looked at the skull from the underside.

The incident had shaken both of them and they were awed by what they had brought aboard. They sat on the seats of the boat with the dip-net between them as they continued to examine the skull. David unhooked his line from the skull and turned on his flashlight to examine the macabre object between them. They both looked without saying anything for a few minutes, their mouths hanging open.

"Look here, Al. This looks like a bullet hole in the back of this skull."

"Damn sure does! Let's get back to shore and take this to the sheriff tomorrow morning."

"The hell with tomorrow morning, we'll take it tonight. I don't think I could sleep with this skull in our camp, thinking about that body down there without one."

"Look for some markers so we can identify this spot. I'm sure they'll want to search for the rest of the body."

Al and David quickly pulled up the anchors and shined the flashlight around to note the location of buoys and landmarks on a piece of paper that Al pulled from his shirt pocket. David brought in the two lanterns and the minnow bucket, then moved to the back and lowered the motor into the water.

"You all set?" asked David

"Let's go," answered Al.

David sat at the back of the boat with his hand on the motor, guiding the boat to the campsite. Al sat in the front with the flashlight, shining it ahead so they could see any obstacle in the water. The skull sat in the dip net between them on the floor of the boat, with the two empty sockets gazing into the night sky.

As they neared the Rhea Springs campsite, they slowed the boat and David jumped from the front into the shallow water with the tie rope in his hand, so he could pull the boat ashore and secure it to the tie down post near the landing. There were approximately ten families in the public access camping area, and they were careful not to awaken anyone when they came ashore. The families had long since gone to bed and the only noise was the splashing they created as they disembarked.

"I hate to wake anybody up this time of the morning," said David as he exited the boat with the dip net in his right hand, the skull bobbing up and down in front of him. He was thinking about the other families in the camping site, as well as his own.

After they'd left a note for their wives, the two men placed the skull, still in the dip net, so they wouldn't have to touch it directly, into the trunk, got into their car, and drove to Dayton, the nearest town in Tennessee.

Both sat quietly, speechless and scared out of their wits.

It was about a thirty-minute drive to Dayton from the campsite and they finally entered the city limits of the town around 3 a.m. The town seemed completely abandoned except for a few passing trucks on their way through town to somewhere else. They found a parking spot in front of the jail and pulled in. As they got out of the car, they saw a deputy come out of the building and they got his attention.

"Can I help you fellas?" the deputy asked as he turned to face them. Deputy Tony Glass was in his early 30s, tall and athletically built, with a full head of blonde hair that he kept impeccably styled in a duck tail. It was rare for someone to be on the streets at this hour and he eyed at them warily, but moved closer. It was obvious that the sight of the two strangers at this odd hour of the morning had put the deputy on edge.

"We've got something that we need to show the sheriff," David answered.

Al moved to the rear of the car and raised the trunk; the David and the deputy followed.

"Holy shit! Where the hell did you boys find that?"

David was the first to respond. "Would you believe that's all we caught fishing tonight?" He felt that humor would help to relieve some of the stress the revelation had created for the deputy. The deputy smiled at the remark and looked at David as if he was unsure what to say next.

Deputy Glass reached into the trunk and took the skull from the net and began to examine it more closely. He rotated the skull under the trunk light to get a better view and placed his pinky finger into the hole on the back of the skull. He then brought it out of the trunk and began walking toward the sheriff's office.

"You fellas come on in and have some coffee. I'm sure the sheriff will want to know how you came onto this."

As they entered the building, the smell of coffee greeted them and the deputy motioned for them to help themselves to some, pointing to a stack of Styrofoam cups and then to a set of chairs before he disappeared through the door with the skull. A short time later, the door reopened and a large, rugged-looking man in his late fifties or early sixties wearing a sheriff's uniform appeared holding the skull in his hands. The deputy followed close behind.

"I'm Fred Robinson, the sheriff here. Looks like you guys had an interesting night of fishing."

Sheriff Robinson could not take his eyes off the skull, and as he talked to the two men, he constantly turned it in his hands. Finally he began to question them more intently.

"Where did you fellas say you came across this?" the sheriff asked as he glared at them across the room.

"We were night-fishing, over close to Rhea Springs, and we hooked it off the bottom of the lake in about fifty feet of water," answered David.

"Kinda rough night for fishin', ain't it? Wind's been sorta brisk tonight." The sheriff was a little skeptical of the two strangers, and they could sense his uneasiness toward them.

Al explained that the two families were on their annual camping and fishing trip when they had hooked into it. He added that they had bought a couple of lots in Toestring Cove, not far from where they camped and explained that they eventually wanted to build summer homes there. He was hoping that the explanation would make the Sheriff feel more at ease with them.

"Alright, so how did you end up hooking this thing?" asked the sheriff as he pointed to the skull that now sat in the center of his desk.

"With the wind blowing us all over the lake, I decided to do a little bottom fishing. Didn't figure it would hurt for the line to drag along the bottom with catfish bait on it, and we certainly weren't catching anything else." David moved forward in his seat as he began to tell the story. His hands were wrapped around his coffee cup as if he needed the warmth from the hot coffee. His eyes lit up with excitement.

"I hooked on a heavy weight and a gob of night crawlers, threw it over the side of the boat. Best I could figure from the amount of line I had out, it musta been about fifty feet to the bottom. My bait bumped along the bottom as the boat moved. The anchors weren't doing much good." He took a sip of his coffee and continued the story.

"After about twenty minutes of bumping along, suddenly my line began to pull and the tip of the rod began to dip. Thought I'd hooked a big cat, so I pulled hard to set the hook and it began to move toward the surface. I yelled at Al to bring the dip net, 'cause I thought it might be hard to bring it in without breaking my line. We were using twenty-pound test line and it felt bigger than that at first."

Al picked up the narrative at this point. "By the time I got to the back of the boat with the net, David already had it close to the top and said he didn't think it was a fish. Said it sort of felt like dead weight. And between the two lanterns, that skull appeared. Let me tell you, a sight like that coming up out of the water is scary as hell."

"Where exactly in this skull was the hook attached when you got it landed? I'll need to let the lab guys know," said the sheriff.

David thought for a moment and then answered. "The hook was caught right under the chin in a little rough place in the bone. The hook was not actually in the skull, the line had passed through that crack and the lead weight had snagged there. I don't think the hook caused any damage. We cut the line off as soon as we got it in."

"Do you remember exactly where you were when you snagged it?" asked Sheriff Robinson.

Al reached into his shirt pocket and pulled out the scrap of paper on which he had written the location. "There was a big triangular marker on the opposite shore on the point that had the number '455' on it. We were probably twenty feet from it. Also, there was a green channel marker to our northwest that was about twenty feet away. Best as we could tell, we were about a half a mile from where we put in at Rhea Springs. That's about as close as I can tell you."

"You think you could look at a map of the lake and locate the area?" asked the sheriff as he opened his desk and pulled out a folded map, and began to unfold it atop a table beside his desk. "These navigational markers are numbered on this map," he said as he put on his glasses and began to study intently. "Let's see. Right here is marker 455, that's on the point there and the green buoy you fellas noted, musta been that one." He moved his finger along the map as he talked, and the two men nodded in agreement.

"That would probably put you somewhere right in this area," said the sheriff as he glanced up at the two men.

"That looks about right," agreed David. "Right there is the boat launching pad at Rhea Springs, and we were camped right there. What do you think, Al?"

"I think that's probably real close," Al said.

"Listen," said the sheriff as he rose from his chair, "I really

9

appreciate you guys bringing this in so quickly. You can bet that there will be a lot of activity up your way in the morning when we start investigating this. When do you fellas plan on leaving to go back to Ohio?"

"We have plans to be here through the Fourth. We always like to spend the Fourth of July here on the lake. One of our traditions," answered Al.

"Well, we'll be in touch if we have any more questions. Once again, thanks for all the information you gave us."

As the two men left the office and walked back out to their car, Sheriff Robinson turned to his deputy. Tony Glass, the chief deputy, had been with the force now for more than ten years. Robinson had been sheriff eight of those years and the two had worked together closely all that time. "Tony," Robinson began, "do you recall any missing persons cases in the county going back a few years?"

"How many years back? It seems like I remember a couple of cases in the past four or five years. One of 'em was a teenager who disappeared, and the other was a wife who also disappeared. Don't recall ever reading that either of them cases was ever solved."

"No, Tony, from the looks of this skull, this case would go back a lot further. I'm no expert, but from the look of the condition it is in, I'd say this one's been down there a very long time."

"So, what are you going to do?"

"I think I'm going to call Sheriff Halford in Hamilton County and take it down there. They got a lot more equipment in Chattanooga than we do here in Dayton. Maybe he can give us some idea as to what we're looking at here. Meanwhile, how about you and Oscar take the boat out in the morning and see if you can seal off the area? We got some floating markers you can put out, and just hang around out there until we find out what we're going to do next."

"I'll call first thing in the morning," said the deputy, "and see if they can meet us at the marker that one of the men mentioned. They've got boats with sirens and lights if we need them."

The sheriff went to his desk and called Hamilton County. After a couple of rings, the dispatcher answered.

"This is Sheriff Robinson in Dayton, is Sheriff Halford in tonight?"

"Yes, sir, he is. Let me get him for you."

After a short pause, Halford came to the line. "Fred!" the sheriff began. "What in the world is going on in Dayton this time of the morning?"

"I've got something very interesting I need you to look at," answered Robinson. "Are you going to be there a while?"

"I'm here for the next four hours at least. What can I do for you?"

"I've got a couple of out-of-state fishermen that found a skull in the lake. Looks pretty old and I thought maybe your lab boys could run some tests and give me a time frame on it."

"Sure Fred, drive on down, I'll go down to the lab and rouse the crew so they'll have everything ready for you. Should see you in less than an hour, then?"

"Sounds about right. I'm on my way."

Purple Haze

Chapter 2
Hamilton County Courthouse
Before sunup, July 1, 1970

It was 5:30 a.m. when Robinson rolled into town and brought his car to a stop in front of the Courthouse. He had placed the skull in a cardboard box, so that he would not draw attention to himself when he came into the building. Off to the side in the sheriff's office, the same dispatcher who initially answered the phone was still on duty.

"Sheriff Robinson to see Sheriff Halford," he said. "I think he's expecting me."

"Yes, sir. Go right on up. I'll let him you're here."

Sheriff Halford was there waiting to greet him. Halford, a tall, imposing figure of a man in his mid-fifties, stood up behind his desk as Robinson entered. Both men had had frequent contact with one another.

"How're you doing, Fred? It's been a while since I've seen you. Have a seat." Halford motioned for him to sit in an old wooden chair. On the right side of Halford's desk sat a Remington typewriter, in the center a thick piece of glass that served as a writing surface piled with papers. To Halford's left was a rotary phone, a flashing white light on the bottom indicating calls as they come in. Halford ignored the calls and asked, "Is that the skull?" pushing aside the pile of papers and

13

pointing to the box.

"That's it, Elmer," he answered and reached into the box to pull out the puzzling item.

The skull was almost black from the time it had spent on the lake bottom, and algae were growing over its top and into the sockets of the eye. It had the strong smell of the lake bottom, and it was obvious from its condition that it had been there a long time.

Sheriff Halford pulled up a chair to the table and laid a clean towel on the top so the evidence could be placed on it. He looked at the piece very slowly and then as he turned it over he saw the bullet hole in the rear of the head. "It's obvious how this person died," Halford said as he pointed to the hole.

"Looks like a murder, for sure," replied Robinson. "Just don't know how long ago we're talking about."

"I guess the rest of the body could answer some questions. You have any idea where it might be?"

"We got some pretty good markers from the two fishermen. They said that they hooked the thing in about fifty feet of water. Going to have to get some divers down there, I'd say."

"Well, let's start with what we've got and see what the lab can tell us."

They left the office and walked down the hall to the elevators and took one of them down to the basement, where the forensics lab was located. As they entered the lab, a small, round man in a white lab coat greeted them. He looked to be around forty years of age, and his neat appearance gave the feeling of someone who cared about himself and about the quality of his work. The lab was immaculate and the chrome examining tables shone brightly in the fluorescent lighting.

The Medical Examiner took out a small scalpel and began to

scrape some of the dark residue from the skull and place it on one of many slides that he had prepared for the study. He also took some of the algae from the inside of the eye socket, as well as some of the dark residue around the bullet hole in the back of the skull. He used a caliper to measure the thickness of the skull and carefully wrote down the dimensions.

"It's difficult to say for certain at this stage, especially without more to go on, but I would guess that this is the skull of a young adult. Probably post-adolescent, maybe twenty or so. Can't tell for certain without the rest of the body or running more tests if it's a male or female. It's also hard to assign a time of death to it except to say that from the algae buildup, the skull had to have been under water for at least twenty years, probably longer. It's fortunate that the mandible was still attached. Maybe we can get an I.D. on it from dental records."

"So, you would guess that I'm looking at a murder that took place in the 1950s or earlier?" asked Robinson.

"I would say that you're pretty close, at least five or six years either way."

"That's still a pretty big playing field," said the sheriff. "How can we narrow it down more?"

"If we had some more parts, we could come a little closer. I'm going to run some more tests, and I should be able to narrow it down in a couple of hours."

"Can you tell anything else about it from what you see?"

The M.E. answered, "Well, it looks like the skull had somehow dislodged from the spine and the rest of the body and that's why the fishermen didn't come up with more. From the look of the base of the skull, it has been dislodged for quite a while. If it were a body that was unearthed or thrown into the lake and weighted down, there would have been a lot of predators feeding, such as turtles, which could have helped the process along. Turtles are real scavengers and they'll eat anything that's on the bottom and not fighting back. Then again, it might have been done during a flood when the lake bed moves more; it's really hard to say."

"We're going to send some divers down tomorrow and see if we can find anything else in the area that might give us a clue," said Robinson. "From the description of the location and where the two men pointed to on the map, it's really close to the old Rhea Springs community. There's still quite a bit of debris from the town there at the bottom of that lake. Should be an interesting hunt."

"What do you want me to do with this skull after my people finish with it?" Elmer asked Robinson.

"Just keep it in a safe place. Hopefully, we'll have more for you to look at by then. Thanks for your time." Robinson shook hands with the M.E. and exited the room with Sheriff Halford.

The two men made their way back to Halford's office.

"How about some coffee, Fred?"

"You got a Coke or something cold?"

"Sure, wait right here and I'll go get you one."

He returned to the office in a few minutes and had the familiar green, embossed bottle in his hands. He handed it to Robinson and after a few gulps, Sheriff Robinson began to discuss the case.

"I've got to get back to Dayton and get the ball rolling on this search we've got ahead of us."

"You got the material to do that kind of search, Fred? That takes some pretty good equipment to dive and search that deep, in that large an area."

"I've got a friend of mine who was a diver in the Navy and he's helped me before. He's pretty good."

"Well, let me give you some advice," Halford said as he swiveled around in his squeaky desk chair to face Robinson. "If he finds anything down there, tell him to mark it where it can be found easily, and try not to disturb it anymore than it already has been. I think I'd call the TVA divers in to recover the body since they own the lake. Might even be a federal case before it's all over."

Robinson sipped on his Coke and mulled over the advice from Halford.

"I guess I'll have to be careful with whatever I find down there. I'll be back in touch if we find any new evidence for your lab people to look over."

Robinson made his way back to his car just as the sun was coming up and the early morning traffic in the downtown area was beginning to pick up. He drove down to a restaurant located on Cherry just off Market Street, and had breakfast and another cup of coffee before heading back to Dayton. As he sat there, he thought about the day ahead, and all the contacts he needed to make when he returned to town. A girl in a tie-dyed t-shirt sat down next to him in the next booth. He thought she looked familiar, but he had too much on his mind to try to figure it out. Before he left Chattanooga, he needed to try to contact his friend, Jerry Standridge, the former Navy diver whom he had mentioned to Halfordl Standridge lived in the Chattanooga area. After eating, Robinson made his way to a pay phone and called his friend after looking up his number in a pocket phone book he kept in his car.

The phone rang four times before a sleepy voice on the other end answered.

"Hello," growled the voice, obviously not happy about having to rise so early.

"Jerry," began the sheriff, "this is Fred Robinson from Dayton. Sorry to have to call so early, but I have something of interest here I thought you could help me with."

"Sure, Fred. What's up?" Jerry began to sound a little more cheerful.

The outdoor pay phone Robinson was calling from was near the restaurant entrance, facing traffic, and the sheriff had to talk louder than normal into the phone. "I've got a situation up here on Watts Bar Lake. I need a diver to help with an investigation."

He held the telephone tightly against his ear and stood as close as he could to the building so that the panels on the sides of the phone booth would shield him from the street noise.

"What are we talking about, Fred? A car accident or something? Did somebody drive off the ferry up there?"

"No, actually, we're talking about a likely homicide."

"A homicide, huh? Well, yeah, I could probably give you a hand."

"Why don't you drive down to the office in Dayton after you get going this morning," Robinson suggested. "I'll fill you in on the details then. This is in about fifty feet of water and we're probably looking at a pretty large area."

"Listen, it would sure help if you could get a hold of some maps from the TVA showing the underwater contours and other features of Watts Bar Lake. I'm not real familiar with the lake, but I know it's one of the first ones they dug in the system. They might even have some elevation maps when they dug the lake back in the early 40s."

"Sure, I'll work on that. I don't really know what we're looking for yet. All we have to go on so far is a very old skull that a couple of fishermen found last night."

"You got water transportation I can use? My boat's in a repair shop right now."

"Sure, Jerry, we'll get you something to use for as long as you need it. You need anything else from me before you come down?"

There was a slight pause before Jerry said, "We'll probably need equipment after we find what we are looking for, but I'll know a little more after I go down and find it. I should be able to get there in a couple of hours after I get my diving tanks loaded up. Let's see, it's seven fifteen right now. How does nine thirty sound?"

"Sounds great," said Robinson as he turned toward the street facing the traffic going by. "I'll get to work on getting you a boat. See you about nine thirty."

"See you then," said Jerry and hung up the phone.

As Robinson got back into his car, he radioed his office. When the dispatcher answered, he asked him to put on Tony Glass, and after a few minutes he came to the radio.

"Hey Sheriff, did you find out anything?"

"Not really," answered the sheriff. "The M.E. down here says the skull is really old and that the rest of the body is still down there in all probability."

"What's your ten-twenty?"

"I'm still in downtown Chattanooga and heading your way." After a short pause, Fred continued. "I need you to contact the marina there and see if we can have use of a large flat-bottom boat, or see if he knows where we can find a barge or something to use."

"That's a ten-four, Sheriff. I'll get right on it. Is there anything else? By the way, I took a couple of deputies out there and we roped off the area with some buoys. The deputies are still there. Also, I talked with a man at the dam and he said that the TVA will send some people out there to assist."

"Call him back and see if he's left yet. If he hasn't, see if he can get his hands on some elevation maps and some maps going back to when the lake was dug out."

"Ten-four. We'll see you in about an hour, I guess?"

"I should be there by then. Radio me back if there's any problems."

Chapter 3
Rhea County Courthouse, Dayton
Mid-morning, July 1, 1970

By the time Robinson pulled back into his parking spot in front of the courthouse, there was already a hornet's nest of activity in town. There were a couple of vehicles parked across the street with TVA logos on them, a black State car parked at a meter on the same side as the courthouse, and a deputy's car hooked up with a flat-bottomed boat. As the sheriff entered the office, he saw Tony standing in front of some TVA maps that were spread out over a table, pointing out locations to the officials. Three uniformed highway patrolmen were walking around in the office asking questions of the dispatcher, a woman in her fifties who had worked at the job for more than ten years, but who seemed to be overwhelmed by this new case. As Robinson walked past, the dispatcher called his name in a pleading tone and he stopped suddenly.

"Sheriff," the dispatcher began, "those two gentlemen from the state patrol said they are here to assist in any way they can."

"Thanks," he answered, "I'll talk to them."

He walked over to the two gentlemen and told them that he could use some help in traffic control from the highway over to the campground, and he would appreciate it if they could help keep away curious spectators. They agreed and said that they would follow and he could show them where he wanted them to set up a road block.

"What are your plans, Sheriff?" asked one of the men from the TVA.

"I've got a diver coming in from Chattanooga in about thirty minutes and we're going to head to the site. You're welcome to come along if you'd like."

"Sounds good," said the engineer as he reached into his breast pocket and pulled out a small note pad and began to scribble notes. He was a small, wiry man in his early 40s with his thinning hair slicked back. "I'm going to call the office and apprise them of the situation. I'll be ready when you are."

The sheriff walked over to where his deputy and some other men from the TVA were poring over the maps. "Tony, how are things going so far?"

"Think we got everything pretty well rolling. Guess you saw the boat outside. Soon as the diver gets here, we'll take him out there. I've got a couple of other guys with boats that made them available to us also."

"Did Jerry Standridge call?" asked the sheriff.

"Hadn't heard from him," answered Tony. "He'll probably be pulling in here any minute, though."

The sheriff held out his hand to the two men from the TVA and thanked them for their help.

The older of the two men spoke. "We're not really sure about what we're up against until we get on site, but from what we have in the way of information, the skull was found close to where the buildings were torn down when the lake was built."

"So there'll be a lot of debris down there?" asked the sheriff.

"Can't say for sure after thirty years, but I would say most of the old foundations are still there, although they are probably covered with river silt by now."

As they were discussing the site, the front door opened and the familiar face of Jerry Standridge entered. Robinson waved him over.

"Good morning, Jerry," said Robinson. "This is my deputy, Tony Glass, and these two gentlemen are with the TVA. They've got a couple of maps here if you want to look them over before we head up there. You can kinda see what you're up against."

Standridge shook hands all around. "How are you fellas doing this morning?" He could feel the tension in the room. "Let's take a look at it and see what's what."

The older of the two men showed him what he had been pointing out to the sheriff. "From what we can see on the map with the information we got from the fishermen, the skull was found in this area." With a red pencil he circled an area that looked to be a half mile in diameter. With a blue pencil he highlighted the area where the town of Rhea Springs had stood before it was demolished for the lake, adding, "This was the main channel of Piney Creek that emptied into the Tennessee River about a mile to the north."

"How deep is this area you have marked in red?" asked Standridge.

"Well, it goes to a depth of about sixty or seventy feet in this area, out to a depth of ten feet or less as you move to the outer areas of the circle."

The TVA engineers told him about the old town that had been there before the lake was built.

"I was telling the sheriff that with the old foundations, silt, and trash, it won't be easy to find the rest of the body."

"So we're looking for a needle in a haystack?"

"That pretty well describes it."

Standridge turned to the sheriff.

"What have we got in the way of equipment to take out there? I saw the boats out front."

"We got a pretty good sized flat-bottomed boat to use as a base of operation and several smaller boats for running errands."

Jerry seemed anxious to get going, and pulled away from the map. "Let's go, Fred," he said to Robinson as they were walking out the door. "We need to get to the site and start the ball rolling. Sounds like this one's going to take some time."

The sheriff followed Jerry out the door toward the car with the boat attached. The two TVA men went to their truck and prepared to follow them to the campground. The procession of two cars and the truck pulling the boat made its way down Highway 27 to Spring City and turned right onto Jackson Street and drove past the high school. It had once been an elementary school which was built during the Depression. They continued for about three miles and turned right toward the Rhea Springs Campground. At this point the sheriff stopped the car and walked back to the state troopers following behind him to tell them to set up a road block at this point. After he got back into the car, he turned toward the campground. The sheriff puffed on a cigar and flipped his ashes out the open window. Jerry and Tony sat quietly, neither speaking. As Robinson began to slow the truck and turn it around to unload the boat at the ramp, the two men came to life.

"Did you already put all your stuff in the boat?" Tony asked Jerry as the truck backed toward the ramp.

"Yeah, I did that before I came into the office. I've got two air tanks. If I need more, I can have someone bring them down to me,"

Jerry explained.

"You fellas get out and untie the boat and float it off the trailer when I back it down," said Sheriff Robinson.

Jerry was the first one out of the truck and he climbed upon the boat and unsecured the tie-down lines and motioned for Robinson to back up into the water. The boat began to float off the trailer as the truck entered the ramp and, holding onto the rope, Jerry guided the boat around the trailer. After the boat was clear and he saw Jerry signal, Robinson pulled the truck off the ramp and parked it in the lot above. By the time he got his gear together, Jerry already had on his diving gear. The three men climbed into the boat and Tony pushed off from the shore. Robinson started the engine on the second pull and guided the boat in reverse away from the ramp. After they had cleared the buoys, he turned the boat toward the diving site. After about fifteen minutes, he slowed the boat and Jerry could see the string of markers that the deputies had put out earlier that set off the dive site.

"How would you like to proceed, Jerry?" Robinson asked.

"I want to start in the middle of the area and work straight out at 90-degree angles toward the outside. We'll anchor the boat in the center so I'll have a focal point."

Robinson moved the boat slowly inside the markers and when he reached the center, he stopped the engine. "Tony, get the rear anchor ready to drop and I'll take care of the front one."

The two anchors slid slowly downward and they were secured to the tie-downs. Before the anchors finished dropping, Jerry had strapped on his tank and put on his flippers. He dangled his mask over the side of the boat and filled it up with water, spit into the mask and rinsed it again to prevent fogging after he entered the colder water. Satisfied everything was in place and functioning correctly, he tightened his mask, waved to the sheriff and eased over the side of the boat into the water.

The two men watched as he disappeared below the boat, and followed his trail of air bubbles as he moved downward. They had brought along a portable radio unit, and the sheriff began to talk into the radio to his office dispatcher.

"Dayton, this is Robinson," he began. "Do you read me?"

"That's a 10-4, Sheriff. Loud and clear," said the female dispatcher, sounding less overwhelmed.

"We are on the site and the diver has already entered the water. We'll let you know if we need anything."

After Jerry entered the water, he swam downward as quickly as possible to get to the working area. He turned on his diving light as he descended and the bottom came into view. Then he moved toward a couple of large rocks off to his right to mark his starting point. A piece of bright plastic tied to one of the rocks marked the spot and Jerry swam slowly along the bottom to the north. As he drifted along the bottom, he slowly moved the debris and rocks to see any evidence of structures underneath. He traveled about 100 yards from the rock and he saw a structure that appeared to be a corner of a building. There were about four courses of brickwork above the bed of the lake, and he dug with his hand to try and see how far the structure went down. As he pulled on the corner, it easily tipped over, so Jerry figured that this was some of the debris from the original buildings, but not one of the buildings itself. Finished exploring this site, he continued to glide along the bottom.

After he had gone another 500 to 600 yards, he retraced his route back to the rock from which he started and continued in the opposite direction, still moving slowly south along the bottom. There seemed to be more rock in this direction and rather than the water getting shallower, he began to swim downward. When he reached the bottom, the lake bed became sandy and leveled off. After moving about 150 yards along the bottom, he came to a base of a building. From the size of the foundation, this appeared to be a large building, and he guessed that he was probably at the site of the old hotel or the school that was near the town. He knew something about the history of the old town that used to stand on the site before they built the lake.

From his granddad's stories, Jerry knew there used to be a large resort hotel in the town of Rhea Springs that was built on the site of a couple of hot springs. People from all over the country used to vacation there. Jerry figured that this would be a good place to do some closer exploring, but not now. He swam another 500 yards and noted the presence of other debris along the rock bluff. He swam back to his starting point and decided to move to the west this time.

He checked his air, and saw that there was still an adequate supply as he moved away from the rock. The bottom in this direction was rather flat and sandy and had nothing worth noting along the way as he swam. He did notice a rather large tree stump with some trash gathered around it about halfway out from the rock, but saw nothing of note.

Fifty feet above, Tony turned to Fred. "How long has he been down there?" he asked the sheriff.

"I figure about an hour now," answered the sheriff.

"How much time does he have in one of them tanks?" asked Tony.

"About two hours or a little better, but he can't stay down that long at that depth, so it'll take him a little longer counting decompression." The sheriff looked at his watch, then continued.

"We'll probably see him in about twenty minutes.""

"Hand me one of them Cokes out of that cooler," said the sheriff. "It's getting hot out here."

"Sure is," said Tony, as he pulled a cold bottle from the cooler.

As Jerry returned to the marked rock, he swam past it without stopping, the last of his first, planned trips. He had not gone far when he realized that in this direction the water was deeper and that it tended to drop off rather steeply for the first few hundred yards. After the bottom began to flatten he looked at his depth gauge and saw that he was at 77 feet. He noted that along the bottom in this direction there were several sites that looked like they could be worth investigating. He especially noted that there were some large concrete structures that looked like they had been parts of buildings at one time. They were too small to be buildings on their own, but they were more than a foot thick and stood a few feet off the bottom of the lake.

He had seen this type of structure before, on a dive in Chickamauga Lake, another of the TVA reservoirs, located in Chattanooga. He had learned that they were forms that were used in the building of the dam and that they had been buried in a deep part of the lake to provide cover for fish and other marine life. He returned to his starting point and then decided to head up and look at some of the maps that the TVA had brought along.

"There he is," yelled Tony, pointing east of the boat as Jerry surfaced about fifty feet away.

Jerry began to swim toward them and Robinson threw over a life ring to pull him into the boat so that it would be easier for him. Jerry caught hold of the ring and the two of them helped him into the boat. As Jerry removed his mask and fins, he sighed deeply as if he were out of breath, then sat back up in the seat to remove his tank and other apparatus.

"Did you see anything down there?" asked Tony.

"A lot of debris and a lot of possibilities."

"Did you see any areas where a body might be hidden or lodged?" asked Robinson

"There are a couple of places," answered Jerry as he looked over the map that was folded on the seat beside him.

"Right here is where I went down, and I went in these four directions," said Jerry as he illustrated with his finger on the map. "There didn't seem to be much in these two directions, but in the south and east, where the water is deeper, there are some large objects and parts of buildings."

"This is where the fisherman found the skull," said the sheriff, pointing to a small 'x' that was marked on the map. "That looks like it's about 100 yards from your starting position toward the shallow water."

"Well, that would make sense," replied Jerry. "If the skull became disconnected and was washed around on the bottom by currents or turbulence, it would probably move closer to the shoreline, so that makes the two areas I suspected as the prime sites to begin."

As Jerry studied the map, his finger retraced the routes that he had taken. He stopped at the deepest area he surveyed, where the concrete forms were located, which appeared to be between the boat and the rock bluff to their right. "Let's put a marker right about there," Jerry told the pair, pointing in the direction where he had gone down. "Make it a different color so we will know where to begin tomorrow."

"What about this yellow marker here?" Tony asked, holding up a smaller buoy that was bright yellow in color.

"That's great, Tony! Get me a spool of nylon to tie to the neck and I'll tie the other end to the concrete form when I go back down."

After Jerry finished his Coke, he prepared his equipment for a second dive.

"Let's move the boat in that direction," said Jerry, pointing toward the bluff. "I'd say, about 200 yards. That way we'll be sort of on top of the area where I want to look."

They pulled up the anchors, and after cranking the engine, moved the boat slowly toward the bluff and dropped the anchors. The rope went down quickly and they estimated the depth to be around 65 feet. By now, Jerry had his gear ready, and after the boat came to a stop and the anchors were steady, he eased over to the edge of the boat to begin his dive.

"Give me that spool of line and I'll tie it off down below," Jerry said as he pointed to the buoy with the line attached.

Tony handed him the line and threw the buoy into the water. Jerry disappeared below the surface with the line in his right hand. As the diver moved downward, the buoy danced on the water then suddenly became still, telling them that Jerry had reached bottom.

Jerry tied the end of the line around a corner of the form so that it would not come loose, then began to swim to the center of the first form. With a small hand tool, he began to dig into the center and found that the form was filled with dirt. He looked along the edges of the form for any loose debris and found nothing. Near the back of the form there appeared to be a cavity that caught his attention. He saw that the cavity was formed from a rotted log that had lodged in the corner and had rotted away, creating a hole between the form and the dirt and rock in its center. He shined his light into the hole and saw nothing.

He moved on to the next form that lay about six feet away. This form was exactly the same size, but it was deeper in the bed of the lake. As he shined his light around the outer edge of the form, he saw a round, metallic-looking object and he picked it up. He was surprised to see that he had picked up a metal button from a military uniform, "USN" embossed on its front. He took out his small digging tool and carefully began to dig where he found the button. He found what appeared to be a belt buckle with the same logo, and then another button. He placed these pieces in a small plastic bag and continued to dig.

He began to widen the area of the dig, then suddenly stopped when he hit against what appeared to be bone. With his hand, he carefully removed the dirt away from a long slender collar bone. Where the neck bone rose to a stubby end, there was a set of dog tags. Jerry removed them and placed them in the bag. At this point, Jerry realized that further digging needed to be done by forensic specialists. He placed the plastic bag into his front pocket and swam toward the boat above.

This time Jerry surfaced on the right side of the boat and reached with his hand for the ladder. As he got out of the water, the two men reached down and helped pull him on board.

"I found the body!" said Jerry excitedly, as he reached into his front pocket and pulled out the pieces that he had collected. He handed them to the sheriff.

"Well, I'll be damned," said Robinson. "Looks like we got us a Navy man down there."

"It looks like the skull became dislodged from the rest of the body above the bed but everything else is down there, as far as I could see."

Sheriff Robinson sounded his air horn and motioned for the boat with the two TVA men who had been waiting outside the search area in case they were needed, to come see what they had found. The other boat moved beside them and Robinson showed them what had been found.

"Looks like we'll have to call the FBI in since this is obviously a military person," said the sheriff as he showed them the dog tags. "They'll probably need to get some equipment in here to remove the body without destroying what evidence is down there."

"What's the condition around the area like?" one of the TVA men asked the diver.

"Well, the body appears to be buried in a large concrete form about ten feet in diameter. The object is probably too large to remove, so the digging will have to be done down there."

"Have you got the area marked so it will be easy to find?"

"I tied that line on that yellow marker to the front edge of a concrete structure that is about eight feet from the body. They won't have any problem finding it."

Chapter 4
Chattanooga, 1941

Kathy Gibson was a twenty-one-year-old, former high school dream girl and had always seen herself as a devoted and loving wife and had worked hard at being a perfect mate for her husband, Larry. A short time after Larry had enlisted in the Navy, she had become lonely and had been seeing Dan Bowers, a former boyfriend. Larry went to the enlistment office downtown in April and had been shipped out to San Diego for basic training. He'd been gone for four months and Kathy wasn't happy about it.

Larry and Kathy had met in high school during their senior year and had gotten married less than a year after graduation. He had played football and baseball and Kathy had been in the band and was always on the honor roll. Larry had insisted that Kathy not work after they were married, to stay home and take care of the house. Larry went to work for his dad, who was a builder, and made a pretty decent living, what with the high demand for starter homes after the Depression years. They were hoping to start a family but their efforts had not resulted in a pregnancy up to the time of his enlistment.

Dan and Kathy had dated off and on before she'd started seeing Larry on a steady basis. Although Dan went to a different school and was three years older, she was attracted to him. He married another classmate of his, Phyllis, after she became pregnant before graduation. They never really dated and the marriage was not a happy one, and even though they managed to hold it together, there was an obvious tension in the house whenever Larry and Kathy visited them. Dan worked the night shift at the U.S. Pipe Foundry, and Phyllis worked day shift in a hosiery mill nearby, so they rarely spent quality time together. Most of Phyllis's time was spent taking care of their now-five-year-old son, Billy.

Kathy was working a few hours in the evenings at Erlanger Hospital each day and found herself free in the daytime, but Larry had a first-shift job at the same foundry where Dan worked nights, so she and Dan began to see more and more of each other. It started innocently, with coffee and conversation while Larry and Phyllis were working, but within a short time, it had become a torrid love affair. Dan and Kathy found in each other what seemed to be missing—the love and closeness—with their own partners, and carried on the affair undetected for almost a year before Larry's enlistment. They were very careful about being together when the danger of Larry coming home was high, such as lunchtime or when the weather turned bad. Since they had neighbors around them who were always "sticking their noses in," they used back entrances and always made sure no one was in the yards around them when they visited. Their houses were next to each other and there was a tall hedge that grew along the back property lines of each lot—the perfect route to go from one house to the other without being seen.

One evening when Kathy was coming home from a four-hour shift at the hospital, Larry confronted her about the problems they were having. He wanted to find out what the problems really were, and why there was so much distance between them.

"Look, babe," he said as he sat with her in the small kitchen and poured her a glass of tea, "I know this is frustrating for you, both of us want to have a child so bad, but we have to keep trying."

He took hold of her hand and looked her in the eyes. She was crying, and he assumed the tears were because of what he had said.. She began to shake uncontrollably. She suddenly came to the realization that she had not been the best wife for Larry, and the guilt of her affair with Dan came crashing down on her.

"I've decided to enlist, sweetheart," he said as he began to cry also. "I feel that enlisting would give us some separation for a while." He looked down at the floor, unable to look her in the eyes, as he continued. "With the war in Europe, I need to go and do my part for the country. We're not at war yet, but there's always the possibility. I really think that a period apart could make our marriage stronger when I return and I would be doing something I really feel strongly about. After I get back, we'll start the family we've dreamed of."

There was no response from Kathy. She took her glass of tea and left the room. Larry stood as she walked out of the kitchen and followed her halfway across the path to the bedroom and sat dejectedly in the small living room staring at the closed door. Nothing else was said by either of them for the next few weeks about the enlistment and they talked very little about anything else up to the day he left.

Larry was shipped out to San Diego on April fifteenth and was scheduled for basic training for three months. After training, he would be shipped to the Pacific fleet, headquartered at Pearl Harbor. Everything went well through basic, and Larry wrote to Kathy almost every day. She did not write as often as he did, but he assumed that she was staying busy and did not have the time to write every day. In July, Larry was transferred to duty aboard the *U.S.S. Oklahoma* in the South

Pacific. The ship left from San Diego and went on assignment at sea. He'd be at sea the next three and a half months, before he'd be able to get a month of R and R in Hawaii at Pearl Harbor.

After her husband was assigned to duty, Kathy began seeing Dan almost daily. Their love affair became intense and there was talk of divorcing their mates and marrying each other. Such talk was very easy for Dan since he and Phyllis had long since stopped any type of intimate relationship. However, it was not as easy for Kathy, who felt that she could not forsake Larry while he was serving his country. She found that continuing the affair with Dan was harder with Larry overseas than it had been when he was home.

One Thursday morning in mid-July, Dan knocked on the back door, and Kathy opened the screen and let him in. He seemed very excited and immediately began to share with her his good news.

"You remember, I told you that Sam Daniels and I have been trying to get on with the TVA?"

"Yea, sure. Did you get on?"

"Sure did, babe!" he answered excitedly, then added, "It's almost twice what I'm making now."

"But that means you'll be working first shift," she said as she poured him a cup of coffee from off the stove.

"I'm afraid so," he said as he made his way into Kathy's kitchen and sat at the table in front of the steaming cup. "We'll have to work a little harder to see each other now."

"How long before you start?" she asked as she sat opposite him at the table.

"They want me at work Monday at Watts Bar."

She arose from the small table where they were sitting and walked over to the cabinet above the stove, seemingly looking for something. It was difficult for her to sit there and look him in the eye while he was talking about the new job.

"Where is that?" she asked, concerned about the sudden change in her routine.

"It's about forty miles north of here. Sam and I are going to carpool with a couple of other guys who got hired." He sipped his coffee. "We'll have to leave about 6 a.m. and will probably be back about 5 p.m."

She turned from the cabinet and looked at him and the concern was on her face as she spoke to him.

"That doesn't leave much time for us."

"We'll have to make what time we have together count." Dan pulled her close and started to kiss her, when suddenly Kathy moved away and turned her back to him. She gazed out the back window.

"I'm afraid I have some news for you, too," said Kathy as she slowly turned to face him.

"What is it?"

"I think I might be pregnant," she said as her eyes dropped to the floor. "I haven't had a period now in three months and I've got other symptoms, too."

"Well, that may just make our decision a little easier," said Dan, as he pulled her close again.

"How does that make it easier?" asked Kathy. She looked up in his eyes and tears began to fall down her cheeks.

"We'll see how this new job works out. I may just go ahead and give Phyllis the divorce she's wanted for so long. I know you're not ready for that move yet, but I think you will be soon."

"I don't know what to do, Dan." She put her arms around him and held him close to her.

"What do you mean? Is there something else?"

"I got a letter from Larry, and he's coming home for a couple of weeks at the end of November. I'll be as big as a house by then!"

"We'll work it out. Quit worrying. Let's make the time we have together right now mean something."

He kissed her softly and the two of them made their way to the bedroom, where their problems disappeared, for a short time anyway..

Chapter 5
Watts Bar Lake Construction Site
October 1941

Dan and his buddy, Sam, were assigned to work with an excavation crew on the lower end of the lake, about a half a mile from the dam itself. They were supposed to help a crew that was digging out one of the lower reaches of the new lake. Sam was paired with a man running a bulldozer, Dan with a dump truck driver, who was hauling dirt from one place to another. The first day on the job was a slow day as they felt their way around and got to know what was expected of them. The work was not hard, but it kept them busy and they had very little free time except at lunch.

They met at the construction trailer after quitting time, punched their time clock, and waited for their two carpool buddies to clock out.

"This is some project," commented Sam. "Looks like most of the excavation is nearly done."

"Yeah, I rode all over the upper end in the truck this afternoon," responded Dan. "When you get out in the middle of this thing, you can't even see to the other side."

"I didn't even realize all this was being done, and they've been working here since July of '39," said Sam as he took off his hard hat and pulled the pocket comb from his pocket and began to comb his sweaty hair.

Dan took a bite from a sandwich he had left in his lunchbox and sipped on some cold coffee from his Thermos.

"I read on the bulletin board over there that they are going to start filling this thing by the first of the year. That's only a couple of months away."

"Oh well," commented Sam, "we'll have a couple more months of good work anyway."

About that time, the other two men walked up, and the four of them walked out to the employee parking lot, got into Sam's Chevrolet, and began the trip back home.

Dan didn't have time to see Kathy that evening. By the time he got home at 5:30, supper was already cooked and he sat down and ate with his wife and son. Billy asked his dad about his new job and Dan told him about all the bulldozers and other equipment. He rattled on constantly with question after question until it was time for him to take his bath and get ready for bed. Dan looked up from his plate and smiled at Billy, who he always seemed to have time for.

"Let's go, young man," chided his mother. "You've got school tomorrow, and you need to get ready for bed. You can talk to your dad about it tomorrow."

"Okay, Mom," answered Billy. "Can you take me up there to see it someday, Dad?"

"Sure thing, buddy," answered Dan. "Maybe we'll drive up there this weekend."

The next morning seemed to come quick, and Dan put on his clothes and went downstairs to eat his breakfast. He was sipping on his second cup of coffee when Sam pulled up in the drive. Phyllis handed him his lunchbox, hardhat, and jacket as he headed for the door.

"See you this evening," said Dan as he walked out the door, happy to be leaving her, but wishing he could say goodbye to Billy before he left.

As they drove to the job site, Sam began to talk about the project and all that had been involved in it since they started. "I wish I had gotten in on this project when it first started," said Sam. "I remember back in '39 when this thing started, we had just had our first child and neither one of us had a job."

"Yeah, I remember the thirties very well myself," said Dan, "I had to drop out of college and go to work after we had Billy in '36. I got a job working on a WPA project downtown. Those were some tough times."

"How'd you get on with U.S. Pipe?" asked Sam.

"Well, they had just landed a big government contract that was tied with making equipment for the Allies. I saw the ad in the paper and applied for one of the new jobs and got on."

"Why did you decide to leave them for this job?" asked Maury, one of the carpoolers.

"This just seemed like a good opportunity and I thought it might work into something long term," answered Dan.

They continued talking about the job and what it could possibly work into until they arrived at the parking lot. There, they got their work jackets, hard hats and lunch boxes and walked together to the construction trailer, where, one by one, they punched in and moved to their designated areas to begin work. Dan waved to Jimmy, the truck driver, and walked towards him. The two of them walked toward the big truck together.

"What are we doing today?" asked Dan.

"We're working around the dam. They've got a bunch of old

forms they used when they built the dam and we're going to haul them," answered Jimmy.

"Where are we taking them?"

"They're supposed to tell us at the dam. Best as I can figure, they're planning on putting them in the bottom of this big hole, and the lake's going to cover them."

The truck moved roughly across the makeshift road in the lake bed toward the dam. Even though it was the end of October, it was a rather warm morning, and Dan sat with his arm out the window smoking a Lucky Strike. As the dam came into sight, they saw where the forms were stacked, and Jimmy turned in that direction. It was an awesome sight as the truck moved along the base of the dam and they looked out the window at the massive structure. It was so high that you could barely see the top of the bridge that went across the dam. Another worker motioned Jimmy to move in his direction, then instructed him to back up to the pile where the forms were stored.

The other worker took out a map of the project and walked over to the truck and began to talk with Jimmy as Dan waited for instructions. "After you load here, take these forms to this site right here." He showed Jimmy where the spot was, and Jimmy nodded that he understood. "They got a small crane there to unload these for you."

"Why are they moving these things there?" Dan asked the man with the map. "Why don't they just bust them up and leave them where they are?"

"This is the most cost-efficient way," answered the man with the map. "It will also provide a natural cover for the fish later. That part of the lake will be almost 70 feet deep."

After the truck was loaded, Dan and Jimmy got in and drove away from the dam and back to the excavation site where they were to unload their truck. After about fifteen minutes of bumpy riding, Jimmy pointed over to his right where there was a small crane set up. It took a little longer to unload the forms than it had to load them, but one by one they were placed in the lake bed about ten to twelve feet apart.

After they were done, a front-end loader came up and dumped a load of fresh dirt into each one to keep them from washing away when the water came. They also drove a large piece of rebar into each corner to keep them in position.

"What's that big, green, triangular sign over there?" Dan asked Jimmy as they were waiting for the crane to unload a form. He was pointing toward a rock bluff with the number 455 on it.

"That's a channel marker for when they fill up the lake," answered Jimmy

"What does it mean?" asked Dan

"I dunno. Probably has something to do with mileage or something. Beats me."

Dan looked at the map as the truck was moving back to the dam for another load. He traced with his finger where the road went that they were on now. It seemed weird to him that all of this would be covered with water shortly.

"This here road," said Jimmy in his Tennessee drawl, "comes out over yonder there close to where they demolished that town. Rhea Springs, I think it was called. It's right over there at the bottom of that next hill. Pretty near a mile and a half or so away."

"You mean there used to be a town there?"

"Yep, there was. It was a pretty good-sized place. They had a big ol' resort hotel and had 'em a couple of hot springs that were supposed to be good for what ails you."

They stopped talking as the crane moved the cable for them to fasten another form. After it had been fastened and the line moved away, Jimmy continued his story.

"From what I heard, folks from all over came here to stay at the hotel so that they could use them hot springs. Folks was pretty upset when the TVA told 'em that the hotel had to go."

"How big was this place?"

"It weren't very big. They had a post office, a school, couple of general stores, the hotel and a couple of churches. Probably had pretty near fifteen or twenty houses around it that had to be torn down. If you look right over thar," said Jimmy, pointing off about a hundred yards beyond where they were unloading the forms, "you can see the old foundation of the hotel."

"Yeah, I see it."

"So this here road goes through where the town was and comes out over thar on the road that you ride in on every day."

Dan looked off in the distance at the dirt road that rose out of the lakebed and made its way back to what would eventually be the shoreline.

"Is this road left open all the time or do they close it off when we're not working here?" asked Dan. He was thinking about his earlier conversation with his son, and was wondering what would be accessible if he brought him up this weekend to look it over before the water came in.

"Naw," answered Jimmy. "They posted some signs up thar but ain't really nobody 'round off hours. Thar's always folks drivin' round down here."

"I noticed that there's not much security up here at night on the site," commented Dan as they climbed back into the truck.

"Thar really ain't much need in guarding a big hole and a bunch of dirt. They got security 'round the construction trailers and at the dam but this out here is wide open." He pointed to a dirt road that went off in the distance. "That thar road goes all the way back up to the paved road that comes into the site, but it's wide open all the way from here to there."

"I guess there's really not much reason for anybody to be up this way," said Dan.

"Every once in a while some teenagers ride out here and camp just for fun, but ain't nobody really gives them a damn."

After another bumpy fifteen minute ride, they arrived back at the dam and got ready to load up another bunch of forms to take to a different part of the lake. They made four trips back and forth from the dam to various sites in the lake bed to deposit the forms. At each site, there was always a dozer to dump gravel, rock and dirt into the form. By the time they had finished with their final load, it was quitting time, and since it was Friday, they were all anxious to clock out and head home for the weekend.

Purple Haze

Chapter 6
Chattanooga, October 1941

Kathy slept in late on Saturday, rising a little before nine, and began to fix some coffee in the kitchen. As the coffee was brewing on the stovetop, she thought about how she was going to face Larry when he came home on leave at the end of November. She even thought about telling him that she had actually gotten pregnant before he left but the timing was not right. He would know that if she had gotten pregnant then, she would be much bigger than she was now, but *maybe* she could fool him into believing she was seven rather than four or five months pregnant. That seemed like the most believable story. She would write in her next letter that she was pregnant and was expecting at the end of December. By the time December got here, he would be overseas and the exact due date wouldn't really matter much anymore. She poured herself a cup of coffee and sat in the quiet kitchen, mulling over her options. Suddenly, there was a knock came at the back door, and she knew that Dan had made his way across the yard to see her.

She greeted him at the door with a big smile and handed him a hot cup of coffee. "Just made this," she said as she handed it to him. "It'll get your motor running."

"I don't need that to get me going." He smiled and looked her up and down. "All I need is you in those flannel pajamas."

He took the coffee from her, placed it on the counter just inside the door, then took her in his arms and held her tightly as he kissed her on the neck.

"Be careful," she warned. "Come on in the house first. The nosy neighbors will see you and then your wife will have some questions for you."

"She worked a late shift last night. She'll be asleep for a while." Dan moved into the kitchen and closed the door behind him and then kissed her, starting at her neck and going all the way down her body, licking her with his tongue as he moved to her sensitive areas.

"Oh, that feels so good," she cooed, as he continued his lovemaking.

She took him by the hand and led him into the bedroom. She pulled the covers back and laid her body down across the bed, with her head on the pillow. She then began to remove her nightclothes and toss them beside the bed. Dan had stripped down to his shorts by the time she had completely removed hers. He lay down on the bed beside her and moved to her as she held her arms out for him. Slowly and passionately, they made love and then continued to hold each other as they enjoyed the afterglow of the moment.

"I don't know what I would have done without you the past few months," she said as she looked into his eyes.

"It's been great for me, too. Believe me! You've filled a void in my life."

"What are we going to do?" she asked as she lay with her back curled against his chest and their hands clasped tightly together.

Dan could feel the tenseness in her, as he began to talk about the situation in front of them. They both had mates they didn't love.

"It's a hell of a situation, babe," said Dan.

"I think I can convince Larry that I am further along than I really am, but sooner or later he is going to figure out that the timing is wrong."

"He won't know until after he gets back," Dan replied.

"I know, but that day will come, and I don't want to face it." Kathy's face showed the concern that was in her thoughts. She looked away, toward the open window, looking at a mockingbird on the electrical wire that attached to the house. She was obviously thinking about the situation that her love affair had created. "What about your wife? Is she serious about moving out?" she asked as she looked back at him.

"She's serious. She doesn't want to be married to me anymore. That part of the puzzle is pretty easy. After I move out, we'll be free to see more of each other with less sneaking around."

Kathy lay still and silent as she thought about what Dan was saying. It was much easier for Dan than it was for her; he didn't love his wife and even though she was obviously enjoying her time with Dan, she still loved Larry. She felt guilty about her relationship with his best friend, but she had to have something to fill the void that he had left. A tear began to roll down her cheek as she lay with her back against Dan. Silently, she got up and sat on the edge of the bed and began to put her clothes back on.

She rose to her feet and faced him as he lay naked across the bed.

"It's easier for you," she said. "You don't have a marriage. Larry and I were okay when he left. We were having some problems, but from the sound of his last few letters, he misses me and he wants to work our problems out."

She went into the bathroom and left him there without saying anything else. When she returned, Dan had dressed and had gone back into the kitchen and was sitting at the table with a cup of coffee.

"It's cold," he said, "but it still takes the edge off." He raised the cup to her as she entered the room. "I know it looks bad to you right now, but it's gonna work out, you'll see."

She sat across from him at the table, cold coffee cup in hand, and shook her head in despair. "I don't think it'll ever work out. I know the truth, and even though I might fool Larry, I can't live with that."

"When is Larry supposed to be back?" asked Dan.

"The last time he wrote, he said he was due for a leave toward the end of November and that he would probably arrive around the first of December."

"That gives us some time to think about the possibilities," said Dan. "I'll come up with something."

"I need to be alone for a while, Dan," she said as she dropped her head rather than look him in the eye.

"Sure, babe. I understand. You let me know if you need me for anything."

Dan rose and placed his cup on the table as he moved to the back door. She was still staring at the floor, and he knew that anything further he said would not be heard.

He closed the door silently behind him as he left.

When she heard the door shut, she rose and looked out to see that Dan had left, then she walked over to the sink, pouring out the remains of the cold coffee. Thoughts ran through her mind, and she did not like the outcome of any of the possibilities. As much as she hated lying and deceit, she knew that it was her only choice. She had been lying about her affair when Larry left, she would just have to continue until he left again for duty. She knew that Larry was very low key and not likely to react violently, but if she told him about the affair, there would be no telling what he might do to her or to Dan. They had arguments before he left for the service and maybe the service had changed him. Maybe she could come clean with him later, after the child was in college or something. She laughed to herself at that absurdity.

"I've got to keep myself busy," she said to herself, "and keep all this out of my mind for a while."

She also had to quit seeing Dan until Larry had been home and left again. She didn't like the way she felt right now and she did not want to keep torturing herself more than she had to. She loved Dan, but making love could wait for a while, for her own sanity.

For the next few weeks, she managed to avoid Dan by being gone when Dan was home after work and on weekends. Kathy was afraid that her feelings for Dan would allow him back into her life at a time when she really needed time alone to work out her problems. So, for her, avoidance was the solution. She went to visit her mother for a couple of weekends, then Larry's mother the following weekend. At Larry's mother's, she learned that Larry's leave had been delayed a week or so and that he wasn't due to come home now until December sixth, and was sure that she would discover a letter waiting for her when she returned home containing the same news.

Larry's mother returned from the kitchen with some iced tea and set it down in front of them on the coffee table. She saw Kathy reading the letter and smiled at her. "I can't wait to see Larry," she said. "It seems like it's been forever since he left."

"It sure does," replied Kathy, "I can't wait to see him." She brushed a tear from her cheek as she looked at her mother-in-law. "I wrote to him last week and told him some news that might make him come home as quickly as possible."

"What news is that, sweetheart?"

Purple Haze

"I'm pregnant."

"Wow!" she exclaimed. "That is really a surprise. When are you due?"

She could hear the wheels turning in Mrs. Gibson's head. Her mother-in-law was concerned that her son was not the father since he had been gone over five months and she was barely showing. Mrs. Gibson looked down at Kathy's mid-section.

"I haven't been to the doctor yet, but I haven't had a period in a while."

"You need to get to the doctor, dear, why don't you use mine? He is really good."

She thought about the problems that would create and quickly answered her. "I'll call my doctor on Monday and make an appointment. I'm much more comfortable with him."

"Are you sure, dear? I could call him now and see if he can come over here."

"No, thank you," she said. "I'd really rather see Dr. Trotter. He's been my doctor since I was six years old."

"Okay, I'm not trying to butt in, just trying to help."

"Thanks a lot, but I'll go tomorrow, I promise," she assured her mother-in-law, so that there would be no cause for suspicion.

"This is so exciting!" exclaimed Mrs. Gibson. "I know Larry will be beside himself when he hears the news."

"You must be what, four or five months along now?"

"That's what I figure," she answered.

"This is really exciting. I can't wait to tell Larry's father."

Kathy took her glass of iced tea and slowly sipped it, as she thought of all the lives that would be affected by what she had done. How was she going to face all of this? There would be a day of reckoning sooner or later, but for now, Kathy just had to figure out how to make it all work until Larry got home.

After her visit, she drove back to her home and went straight to bed. She did not want to turn on any lights, since she didn't know where Dan was at the time and she didn't want to see him right now. As she was drifting off to sleep, she heard a knock at the back door. She knew who it was, and did not want to see him.

Dan began to yell through the door. "Kathy, are you all right?" She could hear the anger in Dan's voice.

Reluctantly, she rose to her feet and went to the back door and cracked it open. "I was asleep, Dan, I really don't feel good right now. Why don't you come back later? I had a rough day."

"You've been dodging me for three weeks now, Kathy! What the hell is going on?"

"Come back tomorrow after you get off work and we'll talk. I promise." She began to pull the screen and close the door.

Dan's foot stopped the closure and he kicked hard against the door after it shut, then jerked it open again and started to come into the kitchen. "Let's talk now," he demanded.

"Please Dan, not now," she pleaded as she retreated a couple of steps. "I'm just not up to it."

He moved from the doorway and she closed the door as his foot cleared the jamb. She breathed a deep sigh of relief as she heard him walk away, but she knew the problem she had created would only get worse and that tomorrow she would have to face it head on.

Purple Haze

Chapter 7
Chattanooga, November 1941

Kathy rose before the sun came up and went to the bathroom to take a long, hot bath. As she lay in the tub with the steam rising around her, she contemplated her next move. She had decided on her way home from the trip to Larry's parents that she was going to have to end her affair with Dan. It had gotten out of control. Dan was spending too much time with her and she needed time to think about her options. She had managed to keep her sanity through all this, but it felt like things were closing in on her now. It was the first day of November, and she knew that Larry would be home the first week of December. She knew from his last letter that he was stationed in Hawaii, temporarily, and that when he returned from his leave with her, he would probably be on the sea again to some far-away port. So far, the war had not involved him, but she read the news and knew that things had been heating up overseas. She thought about how relieved she would be if Larry had to cancel his leave for a while and then she felt guilty for thinking that way.

She rose from the tub, dried herself off, and put on a gown that hung next to the tub. She made her way into the kitchen and put on some coffee on the stove. If she could just end the affair with Dan, everything would be okay. Deep inside, she was beginning to feel uneasy about Dan. Even though their lovemaking was intense, passionate and satisfying, the way he yelled at her last night and tried to force his way into the house made her feel decidedly uncomfortable. Dan, she decided, was not the kind of man who could calmly end an affair. He had already told her about his plans for the two of them after his wife left. She poured a hot cup of coffee, sat silently at the table and began to write out one final letter to Larry before he prepared to come home.

> *Dear Larry,*
>
> *I just got some great news from Dr. Trotter yesterday. I have not been feeling well, so I went to see him. He examined me and told me that I was pregnant. I felt like I might be, having missed my period for a couple of months, and experienced the usual morning nausea. He said that from the way everything looked, that I was probably four or five months along.*
>
> *I went to see your mother yesterday and she was really excited about it, so I thought I better tell you before she did. I wanted you to hear it from me. I really haven't started showing much, and your mother gave me some of her maternity clothes for later. I know this is sudden for you, and I know that you wish you were here for this. I am fine, there is nothing wrong with me as far as Dr. Trotter could see, and I am supposed to go see him again in three weeks.*
>
> *Dan asks about you often. He got a job with the TVA on one of the projects close by. He says that he is anxious to see you and wants you to write him. He and his wife are*

not doing well right now, and I think they are fixing to get a divorce. He brought me a mess of fish the other day that he caught after work. It's been a long time since I've fried fish, but they were really good.

Please write me and tell me when you are coming home so I can make plans to be there to pick you up. The car is running okay. I had to get new points and plugs the other day. A friend of Dan's put them in. The house is empty without you, I miss you. I miss sleeping close to you at night and making love together. Please know that I am counting the days until I see you again.

With all my love,
Kathy

Weeks passed into December before she received a reply from Larry. She had spent the time in virtual seclusion, often with the lights off, to make Dan think she had left town for a short while. She had stopped her mail and was picking it up at the post office to add to the illusion of her not being there. As she went to the post office on one particular day, she had a feeling there would be a letter from Larry and she was right. On top of the pile of mail was the recognizable red, white and blue stationery that he always used. She rushed back to the car, deciding to wait until she got home to open the letter, and was shocked to see Dan, standing beside her car, waiting for her.

"What kind of game are you playing, Kathy?" he asked her as she neared.

"What do you mean?" she asked, trying not to appear frightened.

"I know you've been home every night, but you don't answer your door or your telephone. What the hell is going on?" His voice increased in intensity as he spoke.

"I don't know what you're talking about, Dan. You make it sound like I'm hiding." Kathy was having a difficult time hiding the apprehension in her voice.

"Look, I'll make it easy for you, Kathy. If you don't want to see me for a while, that's fine. Let's make some space for a while. I know you've got a lot going on with Larry coming home. Just promise me that you'll let me know when you're ready to see me again."

Dan's words, clearly meant to reassure her, didn't at all. She still feared what Dan might do to her if things didn't go his way. She reached for the car door handle and dropped her mail, then hastily picked it up.

"I just need to go right now, Dan. I don't want to talk about this out here on the street. Why don't you come over tomorrow evening when you get off and we'll talk about it then?" She hastily slid into the car and rolled the window up and did not wait for a reply.

Dan watched as she drove off, noting a letter that had slid under the car. He waited until she was out of sight, then reached down and picked it up. He could tell from the envelope it was a letter from Larry. He didn't really know what reading the letter would accomplish, but he felt a strong compulsion to read it anyway. It was postmarked November 15, so it had taken almost two weeks to arrive. He opened the letter, removed it from the envelope, breathed in, and read,

Dear Kathy,

It was so good to hear from you and that you are pregnant with our child. You can't begin to know how great it made me feel to know that we are finally going to

be parents after all this time. I have told everyone I know about the news and, of course, everyone has offered suggestions for names. I know this is difficult to go through alone, having to go to the doctor and everything by yourself.

I told my sergeant about it, and he arranged to get me a little free time to come home a little early. I should be home on the first. In fact, by the time you receive this letter, I should only be a couple of days away from you.

I will fly into Chattanooga and catch a bus. I should be there at the latest by 3 p.m. I can't wait to see you and I am so glad we will have this extra week together. Don't have time to write a long letter, but there are so many things I want to share with you when I see you.

With all my love,
Larry

When Kathy arrived home, she was upset to discover that her letter from Larry was not in the mail stack. She searched her purse again and then went out and rummaged through the car, thinking she might have slipped from the stack while driving. Frustrated, she picked up the telephone and called the post office, but the man there assured her that no one had brought in a letter from the parking lot. Then her thoughts drifted back to her confrontation with Dan there. Had he somehow…? The stress of her pregnancy coupled with the thought of losing the letter and him finding it was just too much, and she hurled herself onto the sofa and sobbed.

Purple Haze

Chapter 8
Watts Bar Lake, July 2, 1970

By the next day, word had leaked out that a body had been found at the bottom of the lake. Newspapers from all over the state sent reporters and cameramen, as did news stations from Chattanooga, Knoxville, and Nashville. The campground where the two fishermen had hoped to spend a quiet holiday weekend became a madhouse of hustle and bustle as everyone was trying to get the scoop on the latest discovery. In addition, FBI and Tennessee Bureau of Investigation agents had come in to help with the investigation. For the most part, everyone seemed to know about the skull and the unidentified body it belonged to. The campers at the Rhea Springs site had all heard about the dog tags that had been found and they felt it was just a matter of time before the identity of the body emerged.

Jan Goodson was an attractive 28-year-old reporter for the *Nashville Tennessean*, one of the state's largest newspapers. She had graduated *cum laude* from the University of Tennessee with a major in Journalism. She had worked for local newspapers in the eastern part of the state before being hired by the *Tennessean* as an investigative reporter. She was excited about covering this case which had the potential to become the biggest story in the state that year, as well as help her career. She could see a promotion if she did her job well.

Purple Haze

Accompanying her on the trip was Robert Trent, a forty-year-old photographer and father of two young sons. They'd worked together before on out-of-town assignments, and he'd become a good friend—almost uncle-like—to Jan. Although never married, she had been involved in several affairs with married men that had left her feeling even more alone and was struggling to accept life as an unhappy single. With Robert to keep her focused, this trip was just what she needed to get her mind off her personal problems and get ahead at the *Tennessean*.

Access to the site was restricted, and the few reporters who had managed to weasel their way in were at the campsite begging for news like starving dogs for any scrap available. Strewn about were several news vans from Chattanooga stations and one from a Knoxville station. She recognized several newspaper reporters walking aimlessly from van to van, including one from the small local paper.

"Get some shots of those Feds over there," said Jan to Robert, pointing in the direction of two men climbing aboard an aluminum boat. She knew they were federal agents because she had observed them going back and forth to a black government vehicle.

They moved hastily to the water's edge and began to snap pictures of the two men. After they had several dozen shots, Jan moved in to question them. The two men were busily involved in loading material aboard the small boat.

"Good morning gentlemen. Jan Goodson, from the *Nashville Tennessean*. May I ask a few questions before you push out?" she asked politely.

The younger of the two men moved forward. He put out his hand to greet Jan and Robert as they walked down the ramp closer to the boat.

"I'm Bryan Langston. This is my partner, Joe Mallory," he said, pointing to the older man.

"Have you been to the site yet?" asked Jan.

"No," replied Langston. "We just arrived this morning. This will be our first trip out there."

"Do you know the name or any other information about the victim?" asked Jan.

She could sense that the agent was looking her over, so she gave him her best smile and inched closer to the boat on the ramp. Leaning suggestively against the post at the edge of the water, she thrust a hip towards him to show off her thin, sensual form. It was a posture that any man, including the agent, would find hard to resist.

"Not at this time, but I am sure that when I return this afternoon, I will have a lot of basic information that will allow us to fully begin our investigation." He turned his eyes away from the motor that he lowered into the water, and focused entirely on Jan as he finished talking. "Why don't you look out for me at lunch time and we'll ride into Dayton and I can show you what we've got then?"

"Great!" replied Jan excitedly. "We'll be looking for you around noon."

As the two men pushed off, Jan and Robert watched them.

"Looks like you made a good contact there, Jan," commented Robert as he smiled at her slyly. "Sometimes it helps to have more than a stenographer's pad when you're trying to find out something."

"We'll see," said Jan. "We'll definitely see."

It took the pair of FBI agents about twenty minutes to arrive at the crime scene and they eased their boat into the flotilla that had gathered there. Mallory was driving the boat, so Langston stood in the front as they neared and showed their IDs to the deputy in charge of policing the area.

"Bryan Langston," he said to Tony Glass, "This is my partner, Joe Mallory, we're with the FBI. Can you direct us to the dive site?"

"On that flat-bottomed barge you will find Fred Robinson. He's the sheriff here. I'm sure he can fill you in." Deputy Glass pointed in the direction of the large operations barge that had been set up.

Mallory pulled the start rope on the twenty horse engine and the boat moved slowly toward the barge that was anchored in the middle of the crime scene. As they neared the barge, they could see the sheriff was talking to a diver who had just surfaced and was handing some materials to the sheriff as they neared. Langston could hear part of the conversation as they pulled beside the barge which had been sent to the site by the TVA. It was about thirty feet long and looked to be about fifteen feet wide. There were ladders attached to the side near the tie-ons for the boat. They tied both the front and rear of the boat to prevent it from moving around and getting damaged by the metal barge.

"This was lying about ten feet from the form," the diver said as he handed the sheriff a large metal object.

"Looks like an old pocketknife," said the sheriff. He turned the metal object around looking for some kind of marking. "Can't see anything that looks unusual," he said as he placed it in a plastic bag. "Just the same, we'll send it down to Chattanooga with the other stuff."

"Sheriff Robinson?"

The sheriff turned to face Langston, who had made his way up to him. "What can I do for you?" asked Robinson.

He introduced himself and his partner. "We're with the FBI and we've been sent here to assist in this investigation. We understand that the body is that of a member of the U.S. Navy."

"That's right. Come over this way," instructed the sheriff, "and I'll show you what we have come up with so far."

There was a long bench set up in the center of the barge that had the various pieces, excluding the skull, spread out. Every time another piece surfaced it was placed on the bench with the others.

Mallory picked up one of the hexagonal dog tags. "This is Navy. It's a steel-nickel alloy that they used in the early 40s. They used this combination so the tags wouldn't rust or corrode. The shape cinches it."

Langston took out a notepad and began to copy down the information embossed on the tag. "I'll call this in to Washington, and we should be able to dig up some information for you soon."

"The name is Lawrence Gibson," Mallory said, squinting at the etched letters. "Looks like he enlisted in 1940, and was in the Pacific somewhere. That's about all I can tell from just looking at it." Mallory wrote down all the pertinent information, and picked up a couple of the uniform buttons that lay there. "This button style would also put him in that time period."

He turned to Sheriff Robinson, shielding his eyes from the morning sun that was peering over the tops of the trees. "We'll call in some Navy divers and some forensic people to help investigate what we have here. Tell me what you've discovered so far."

"Our diver found a large concrete form that was submerged when the lake was built in the early 40s and filled with large rocks. The body was buried in that form beneath those rocks. After all these years, the head worked itself free and was discovered by two fishermen. When our diver went down, he found the forms and located the one the head came from."

Langston and Mallory began to walk around the display that had been spread out on the table. There was a wide assortment of items, everything from pieces of uniform and shoes to bone fragments and other currently unidentified things. Mallory seemed engrossed by the fragments of the uniform, the dog tags, and pieces of what looked like the sole of a shoe.

"You know, Joe," began Langston, "if this guy was stationed in the Pacific during the war, wonder what the odds would be that we could find him on an MIA list somewhere out there? Think about all the guys that were lost at sea and never recovered. I would be willing to bet that he was from this area, and his family thinks he was killed in the war."

"Might be. I'm gonna take some pictures of this stuff, and get the information off the dog tags. See if we can begin finding out something about the victim." Mallory moved around the table and began to take close-ups of the evidence. He was using a Polaroid Land Camera, and as the pictures were spitting out of the front of the camera, he was taking them out and shaking them in the air to speed up the drying before sliding the photos into his jacket pocket.

Mallory and Langston worked for the rest of the morning shooting photographs of the artifacts and looking at the evidence on board the barge. As they worked, they would occasionally ask questions to the diver as he came up for breaks. After they had sifted through all that was available, they decided to go back to shore for lunch and come back in the afternoon. Langston was especially eager to get back to the launch site because of the promised lunch he had given that nice-looking reporter.

As they pulled the boat back upon the land at the launch site, they did not see the pair of reporters who talked to them as they left for the barge earlier. They pulled the last of their equipment out of the boat and loaded it into their car. But just as they were preparing to leave, they heard a woman's voice calling to them.

"Hey, you two!" Jan yelled, as she came running up to the side of their vehicle.

"I was looking around for you," Langston said. "Didn't see you, so we were thinking of taking a drive around the camp to look for you before we drove into Dayton for some lunch."

"Yeah, we were over there talking to some of the deputies and onlookers when you came up," said Jan.

"You hungry, Jan?" asked Langston.

"I'm famished," she answered.

"Why don't you yell for Robert and the four of us can ride into Dayton and get some lunch? I hear there's a pretty good diner downtown that has real home-cooked meals."

"Good idea, then you can fill us in on what's going on out there."

Purple Haze

Chapter 9
Dayton, Early Afternoon, Same Day

As they pulled within sight of the courthouse, Jan told the pair about some of the history associated with the town. She knew quite a bit about the town's history and she was trying to impress them with it. An impressed Fed was a talkative Fed, or so she hoped.

"You'll have to forgive me, I started out as a history major in college, and the story of this place has always fascinated me," she said. She pointed out her window to the big brick building on their right.

"That's the courthouse where they had the famous Monkey Trial. Ever heard of it?" she asked.

"Yeah" answered Joe Mallory. "I remember that story from my high school history class. Something to do with the teaching of evolution."

"Gold star for Joe," quipped Jan. "That trial put Dayton in the national news about this same time back in the twenties."

She pointed to a large, two-storied frame house across the street and continued her lesson. "Right there in that house is where William Jennings Bryan stayed during the trial and he died there. They have a college in town named for him."

As they rolled past the courthouse, Bryan Langston pointed to a street diagonally across from the brick structure. "Turn left on the next street. There's supposed to be a good eating place down there on the right called the Southern Grill."

They found a vacant parking spot nearby and walked back to the crowded diner, obviously a popular spot with the locals. They made their way through the door and a waitress took them to a table near the rear of the diner and handed them each a menu. The delicious smells of the menu items wafted on the air and made them even hungrier.

Joe and Bryan ordered chicken and dumplings with a couple of vegetables; Jan and Robert both ordered pork chops with apples and green beans. As they were waiting on their food, they began to discuss the events of the day.

"I hope you don't mind," Jan began, "if I take a few notes while we talk. I don't want to forget any of the details you guys give us."

"No, no, of course not," replied Joe. "You take all the notes you need."

"What exactly did they find out there?" Jan asked.

"They found out that there was a body buried under the lake in an old construction form that was used to build the dam in the forties," responded Joe.

"Do they know who the person was or anything else about him?" she asked.

Joe removed the Polaroids from his jacket pocket and handed them across the table to Jan. He and Bryan explained the information they had been given. At the end of their description they told her that the body had been identified as a Lawrence Gibson. Jan wrote down all the information they were giving her.

Jan looked at Bryan in amazement as she asked, "So, you're saying that this person was killed thirty years ago?"

Joe began adding some detail to the timeline as they knew it at that time. "According to the TVA guy who was out on the barge this morning, they began filling this lake in early December of 1941, and had it completely full by the first part of February. Seems they had some flooding at that time, too. That made it a little easier to fill the reservoir."

The waitress arrived with their food. For a short time, conversation stopped. After they'd eaten for a few minutes, Bryan continued with the ideas that they'd come up with concerning the murder.

"I would guess that the murderer had to be someone who either worked at the TVA site when the construction was going on, or someone locally who knew about the details of the lake construction. It's going to take some real digging to come up with any suspects after all this time."

"What other evidence did they come up with from the lake? Was there anything that might tell us where this person was from?" Jan asked.

"We'll be able to come up with more information from the U.S. Navy when our people do a trace on the dog tags. Should be able to tell us where he was from and where he was stationed," Joe added.

"While you were out at the dive site, we talked with the two guys who found the skull," Jan offered.

"Man, you could tell from just talking to them that those guys were really scared when they fished that skull out of the lake," said Robert. "They talked about how neither one of them could think straight after they got it aboard the boat. It sounds like it really freaked them out when they found the skull. They said that they were really unsure about what to do with it, but they finally decided to take it to the sheriff. Apparently, they actually thought about just throwing it back in the water but decided that they needed to take it to somebody that could investigate where it came from. I got some pretty good shots of the two guys that we can use for our lead story in tonight's edition, or at least in the early morning one," Robert said.

"If we can't get the pictures in time, we can at least do a pretty exciting story with the information that you guys have given me." Jan smiled, excited about getting the story in as quickly as possible.

"Well, we've got a lot of questions to answer, and I'm sure," said Bryan, "that as we uncover more of the evidence from the dive site and find out who this guy was, we'll be able to zero in on when he was killed and possibly why he was killed. Should be an interesting search."

As they finished their meal, they began to push away from the table and Jan reached out and took the check from the waitress. "This one's on me, guys. Just keep giving me the information as you can come up with it. It's well worth it."

Chapter 10
Chattanooga, December 2, 1941

Kathy had spent a few nights at her mother-in-law's house and was trying to stay away from her own house as much as possible to avoid Dan. Visiting with Mrs. Gibson helped her to bring Larry closer and since she had gotten the letter from Larry, she tried as much as possible to keep her distance from Dan. Within the past month, he'd become very possessive, and it seemed that he was always around. His situation with Phyllis, and living in a motel, had made it more difficult for him, but made it even harder for her. She had to focus on Larry's return, so staying with Larry's mom seemed to be the easiest thing for her to do. She had also been out of town a couple of times with her friend Beth, whose husband was also overseas. The two of them had taken a trip a couple of weeks earlier to visit Beth's parents who lived on a large farm in Athens, Tennessee, an hour or so north.

Kathy awakened early, just as the sun was rising, and tiptoed into the kitchen to put on a pot of coffee. As she was waiting on the coffee to heat on the stove, she sat at the table and read through the last letter she had from Larry, not including the one she'd lost after running into Dan at the post office. She wondered what the lost letter had said as she read the line about Larry's return on the 6th. It was less than a week away before he would be home. She looked out the kitchen window at the sun rising over the tops of the trees and imagined what it would be like to see him again. She felt so guilty that she had not remained faithful to him, and was determined to make it up to him. She wiped her eyes with the cuff of her nightshirt before taking a cup out of the cupboard. Since Larry had gone away, she had learned to drink the coffee black; the rationing programs that had been put into place because of the war made sugar one of those things she could do without.

She took her cup of hot coffee and saucer to the front porch and sat in the glider Mrs. Gibson had facing the street eastward toward the rising sun. Following the death of Larry's father, his mother had bought the house and continued to live in it alone. It was situated on about an acre of land in the middle of a housing development that had been built with WPA funds in the late 30s. The house was a white two-story with a large front porch, and steps leading down to the street. There was a rail line in front of the house so that Mrs. Gibson could catch a cable car into town whenever she wanted to go. She had a grocery store on the next block and her church was just around the corner, so she had never really needed a car. It was a clean, quiet neighborhood, about fifteen minutes out of town.

Mrs. Gibson had installed a metal awning on the front of her house so the sun would not hit her in the eyes, but Kathy still squinted, thoughts of Larry's return running through her mind. She didn't notice her mother-in-law's arrival until the woman touched Kathy's shoulder.

"Well, good morning," she said cheerfully. "You're up awfully early."

"I just thought I would greet the morning."

"Would you like company?"

"That would be nice."

Kathy sat in the glider and watched as the lights across the street and the neighborhood slowly came to life.

"It's a little cool out here, Kathy. Are you sure you don't want to move to the parlor?"

"I would really rather stay out here in the fresh air, if you don't mind. It's a little stuffy inside."

"Well, that's fine, too, darling." The woman paused, then mentioned, "We're just a week away from Larry returning. You must be excited about seeing him."

"Yes, ma'am. Time seems to be dragging since I last heard from him."

"Well, I know that Larry will be glad to see you and to talk over the plans for the baby with you." She took a sip of coffee, and continued. "Maybe you can think of a name together while he's here. Of course, you'll have to think of a boy's and a girl's name."

"I'm really excited about seeing him. I know he'll be thrilled about the baby and being a father."

The two sat quietly for a few minutes. Finally, Kathy stood and faced Mrs. Gibson.

"I would really like to stay here with you until Larry comes back, if you don't mind. It gets so lonesome at home without him." Tears were beginning to show as she continued. "I feel closer to him, here with you."

"I was going to suggest that myself. Looks like you beat me to it. I'd love to have you stay."

Mrs. Gibson stood and the two embraced for a few minutes.

"Thanks, I really needed that," Kathy offered.

Mrs. Gibson looked fondly at her daughter-in-law and suggested that they could go to Kathy's house and pick up a few things. Kathy agreed, asking if they could stop at the store on the way back so she could pick up some additional items.

"It'll do us both good to get out and about a bit," Mrs. Gibson , as the two walked together, hand in hand, back into the house.

Chapter 11
Chattanooga, December 3, 1941

Dan was becoming impatient. He had been over at Kathy's house three times now and not once caught her at home. He was beginning to think that she had left town. Over a month had passed since his encounter with Kathy outside the post office. He saw a car stop in front of the house, just as he started to pull out of Kathy's driveway. Neither the car nor the woman who was walking up the steps toward the front door was familiar to him, but she must have known Kathy, so he got out of his truck and walked over to her.

"How do you do, ma'am? I'm Dan Bowers, a friend of Kathy and Larry's." He held out his hand for a greeting. Beth took it and shook hands cautiously.

"Good to meet you, Mr. Bowers. I'm Beth Miller. I just live around the block and I came by to visit. I guess she must be out, huh?"

"Any idea where she might be? I really need to see her about Larry coming home."

"No, I have no idea. I know she had a doctor's appointment this morning, maybe she already left for that." She knew that Kathy was probably over at Mrs. Gibson's, but Kathy had told her about Dan.

"I'll check back tomorrow," Dan said. "If you see her, tell her I dropped by."

"I'll do that," said Beth. She watched Dan get back into his truck and drive away, then she drove over to Mrs. Gibson's house. As she drove she became very uneasy about Dan being there and was not sure that she would tell Kathy about meeting him. It would only worry her needlessly and that wouldn't be good for the baby.

She drove on, unaware of the truck that was following her, some distance back.

The truck was careful to stay on Beth's car, far enough back to not be obvious to her. They drove through town and all the way out to the Brainerd area, on the opposite side of town from where Kathy lived. Beth stopped her car in front of a white frame house. The driver stopped his truck far enough away to not be seen, and wrote down the address on a piece of paper, before turning around and driving back to the motel.

Beth knocked at the front door, and heard the sound of footsteps coming down the stairs and toward the door. The door opened and Mrs. Gibson stood there and greeted her. "Good evening, Beth," Mrs. Gibson began. "It's good to see you again. Come on in and sit down, I'll call Kathy down for you."

"Thank you, ma'am," said Beth as she walked into the parlor and sat down.

"Hey, Beth. What brings you way over here?" Kathy asked as she sat across from her.

"Can we go out on the front porch for a minute?" Beth asked as she took hold of Kathy's hand with her own shaking hand, "I need to talk with you about something—alone if I can."

"Sure, let's take a walk around the block, I need a little exercise." Kathy could sense the tenseness in Beth's voice and the obvious shaking of her hand as she held it

As they walked down the front steps and onto the sidewalk, Beth began to talk. "I met Dan Bowers today." She looked her friend in the eyes and could see the concern on her face. "I wasn't going to tell you but I thought you should know that he was at your house, in case you had to go by there for something."

"Oh, no! When?"

"I went over to your house this afternoon to see you and his truck was there. I didn't know it was him or I would have just kept going."

"What did he say?" Kathy asked.

"He wanted to know if I knew where you were. I told him you had a doctor's appointment." Beth's voice was tense and her eyes seemed to go here and there instead of focusing on Kathy. Beth's eyes moved up and down the streets as they walked, looking for the truck that she had seen.

"Do you think he believed you?"

"Well, I stayed there until he drove away," Beth answered, "but he didn't seem to be satisfied. He told me to tell you that he had dropped by."

"No, he's not satisfied. I think it's just a matter of time until he finds out that I'm here. He never really knew where Larry's parents lived, but I'm sure he'll ask around and find out."

"What do you want to do?"

"Well, let's figure out something tomorrow, while he's at work. I'm really afraid to be around him right now." She began to think over the possibilities, and then continued. "Why don't we go up to your folk's place until then? He'll never find us there, and Larry will be home and we can figure out what to do next."

They decided to take Kathy's car and to leave mid-morning the next day while Dan was at work. They talked about spending the time at Beth's parents' home in Athens, and driving back after Larry got home on leave.

"Do you know exactly when he is coming in?" Beth asked her.

"I checked the bus schedules. I'm not really sure whether he is coming into town, but I know his leave starts on the 6th. I'm guessing he'll leave Hawaii on the 6th and get home late on the 7th, so that's what I'm counting on. There's a bus due to arrive mid-day on the 7th."

"What are you going to tell your mother-in-law?" asked Beth. "You don't really want to upset her."

Kathy stopped walking for a few seconds and turned to face Beth. "I'll just tell her that you offered to take me out of town for a few days, and that I will be back on the 6th."

"I'm sure she'll understand."

On the walk back to Mrs. Gibson's house, they decided to not wait until the next morning and to go ahead and make the trip now. They decided to load up Kathy's clothes from her mother-in-law's and to head north to Beth's parents in Athens.

The two of them walked back to the house, explained the situation to Mrs. Gibson and loaded the stuff in Kathy's car. Kathy told Mrs. Gibson that Beth was having a difficult time and that she needed to drive up to her parents' home and had invited her to go along. Then Kathy followed Beth back to her house. Beth went in the house and threw a few things into a suitcase and came back out, tossed the suitcase into the backseat, and they took off.

"Don't we need to call your parents, and make sure they're home?" Kathy asked as they backed out into the street.

"They don't have a phone on the farm, and they never go anywhere anyway. They'll be there. Don't worry."

By noon, they were pulling off the highway on the dirt road

leading to Beth's parents' home.

Purple Haze

Chapter 12
Chattanooga, December 6, 1941

Dan was becoming more and more frustrated. He had been watching the house every afternoon when he got home from work, and there was no sign of Kathy or her car. He had driven by Beth's house several times also, and her car was always there, too. He needed to see Kathy, but it was important that he kept out of sight as long as possible. The time was fast approaching that Kathy expected Larry to be coming home. He was sure that if he stayed around long enough, he would be there when Kathy discovered that something had happened to Larry's leave and that he wasn't coming home at this time. He needed to be close by for her.

While Dan was watching her house, Kathy and Beth were settling in with Beth's parents and for the first time in more than a month, Kathy was able to relax and momentarily at least, forget about Dan. She was focusing on what she would do when Larry returned.

It was really strange living so long without electricity or running water. Like most of the people who lived in these rural areas, there were no conveniences that had become so commonplace for them living in Chattanooga. As Kathy spent more time living without those things she could not help but think about how the opening of the TVA dams and power plants was going to be a real blessing to people like

Beth's mother and father.

One day while they were there, the TVA had set up two huge tents on the outskirts of Athens. In one tent, the people could come by and see the new electric appliances that they would soon be able to use in their homes. And in the other, they had speakers, including Tennessee Senators Albert Gore and Estes Kefauver. They had preachers from nearby churches and some gospel singers. In addition, they had talented country and bluegrass performers who traveled around with the show, including an eighteen-year-old picker and singer named Buck Owens.

It was nice to spend the day seeing all the modern appliances, and Beth's mom and dad bought an electric stove and a new refrigerator. It was a carnival-like atmosphere and there were concession stands where you could buy cotton candy and popcorn. After the show ended, Kathy talked to Beth about their plans.

"I guess we had better head home tomorrow," she began. "I'm sure that Larry will be home, I just don't know what time he's coming."

"We can leave after breakfast in the morning and drive straight to your house," Beth agreed. "We should get there late enough to miss Dan, and early enough to be there when Larry calls you."

After they got back to the house, Kathy told Beth's mom about their plans and thanked her for putting up with them for the past few days.

"Next time," Beth's mother said, "I'll be able to cook you something on my new electric stove. Sure is gonna be nice to have all them fancy electric things."

The morning of the 7th, Kathy got up early and had breakfast with Beth and her parents. Her father was always getting up early to milk the cows, so they got to say goodbye to everyone before they left.

By 8 a.m., they were pulling into the driveway that led into Kathy and Larry's garage. They entered the house and began to unpack their things from the car.

"I'm going to walk over to the house and get the car and drive it back over here to get the rest of my things so I won't have to carry that suitcase and the rest of my stuff up the street," Beth said.

"I don't mind running you over there," argued Kathy. "That's a pretty good walk."

"No, it's just around the block," Beth said, "and I need the walk."

"Well, by the time you get back," Kathy said, "I'll have some coffee on for us and we can listen to the radio while we're waiting for Larry's phone call."

"That sounds good. I'll be back in a short while." Beth disappeared around the corner, walking back to her house, and Kathy went inside to put on some coffee.

Dan had already been told that he had two more weeks of work left on the Watts Bar project but was offered a job working on a similar project below Chattanooga at the Hales Bar Dam. The Hales Bar Dam had been built all the way back in the early 1900s and had been bought out by the TVA, which had discovered that the dam was built on a weak limestone base. They were supposed to repair the damage, install a more substantial foundation and modernize it. It was entirely different from the work he had done on the Watts Bar project, but the work would be steady. He wasn't sure if he wanted to take the job or not, but he had to do something to make money. He wasn't ready to just quit working, so he had to come to work every day, even though his mind was always on Kathy. He thought to himself that someone had to be there to pick up the pieces, and he planned to do just that.

Sam had told Dan that he planned on taking a job at Hales Bar and that they could continue to ride together. It was unusual to have to work on a Sunday, but there was a deadline to complete this particular phase of construction so a crew was working. As usual, the crew (what was left of it) was sitting around the construction trailer having an afternoon break, and listening to the radio that played through the open window of the trailer. Right after they had started their break, they interrupted the program with an important announcement.

"The Japanese have attacked our military installation on the island of Oahu, also known as Pearl Harbor."

According to the broadcast, several battleships had been hit, as well as troops and buildings on the island. For the rest of the afternoon, the bombing was all anyone, Dan included, could talk about. But as they all returned to work, another thought occurred to Dan. The bombing was just what he needed. Now there was an explanation for Larry not showing up at the bus station today. It would be logical for Kathy to think that he, too, had been killed. Dan could not help but think about how the tragedy of all those men dying in that bombing had created the perfect cover for explaining why Larry did not show up for his scheduled leave.

Kathy and Beth were drinking their second cup of coffee listening to church announcements on the local radio station, WDEF-AM in Kathy's parlor when they heard the same announcement. An 18-year-old part-time announcer named Luther Massengill ripped off a teletype and sat down in front of the microphone and read it off to his audience.

"The Japanese have attacked our military installation on the island of Oahu, also known as Pearl Harbor."

"Oh, my God!" Kathy cried, dropping her cup and saucer on the floor. "I hope Larry got out of there before that happened."

Beth rushed over from her seat to the couch and put her arm around Kathy's shoulder. "I'm sure he did, Kathy," she said comfortingly. "He'll be calling any minute."

"Oh, God! I hope you're right" Kathy said, sobbing. "I've got a really bad feeling about it right now."

Kathy listened to the short broadcast intently as they mentioned that several battleships were sunk by the Japanese bombers and that many Americans had died in the bombing. She had no idea which ships were sunk, but she knew that Larry's ship, the *U.S.S. Oklahoma*, was in the harbor.

"Why don't we go down to the bus station and wait on his bus to come in?" suggested Beth. "I'm sure he'll be coming in."

Kathy thought about it for a moment and then said, "No, I need to stay here by the phone. Someone may be calling me soon, or Larry will call when his bus comes in."

"You're right," agreed Beth. "I'll stay here with you and wait it out."

The day crept by slowly. She called the bus station three times to find out about any westbound buses that were coming in, but Larry's name was not on any of the passenger lists. As the day wore on, Kathy became more and more convinced that Larry was not returning. Radio reports that came in got progressively worse throughout the day. She was unable to eat anything, in spite of all the pleadings from Beth.

"You have to eat something. Think about the baby."

She tried to keep her composure as long as possible, but she spent the evening in a state of flux. She really didn't know what to do next, and she convinced herself that the phone was about to ring, so she refused to leave it. The silence was broken just before dark with a knock at the back door. Dan was waiting for her in the doorway.

"Is Kathy okay?" he asked Beth as the door opened. His face showed a real concern for Kathy, but Beth was uneasy about his presence.

"No, Dan." Beth answered. "She's having a really hard time right now."

"Okay," Dan said. "Please tell her I dropped by, and that she can call me at the Alamo Plaza if she needs to talk. Room 117."

"I'll tell her you were here."

She watched as Dan walked down the back steps and out into the driveway, got into his truck and drove away. Knowing how Kathy felt at the moment, she was hopeful that she did not hear the conversation, or realize that he dropped by. She would deliver Dan's message, but not today.

A couple of days passed and still there was no word from anyone concerning Larry or the plight of his ship. Following the speech of President Roosevelt before Congress, declaring war, Beth, too, knew that her own husband would be in danger and she tried her best to be supportive of Kathy and not worry about her husband overseas.

Kathy made trips each day to the newspaper office downtown and received updates from time to time, but there was not much in the way of names or identities. On one of her trips, she found out that the two ships that received the heaviest losses in fatalities were the *U.S.S. Arizona* and the *U.S.S. Oklahoma*. Larry's ship. She knew that if his leave had been delayed by just a few hours that the chances were good that he was still on the ship when the Japanese attacked. In one report, she read that 429 men aboard Larry's ship had died and that 32 survivors had been rescued from the damaged hull. Those survivors had yet to be identified, so there was still hope for her that he was among them or still in transit for his scheduled leave.

Chapter 13
Crime Recovery Scene, July 3, 1971

After lunch, Bryan and Joe, along with Jan and Robert, drove back out to the dive site. When they drove up, it seemed that the crowd around the lake had gotten larger, and it was difficult to park the car as closely as before. They were amazed that word had gotten out so quickly, and that so many people from such a small town had gathered.

"It's totally amazing," began Joe, "how catastrophe brings people out of the woodwork."

"It's crazy," Jan replied. "I mean, hell, it's the holiday weekend. You would think all these people would have something to do."

"This is the best entertainment there is," said Bryan. "How many times do you think these people would get to witness a real crime scene? It's a lot better than TV."

Robert began walking through the crowd and getting some photographs of the people who were standing around to go with Jan's article. Jan turned to Bryan and Joe as they were preparing to go back out on their boat and asked him if they could come out to the site with them.

"I wouldn't have any problem with it," answered Bryan, "but that boat is awfully small for four people."

"Maybe we can rent a boat or something," said Jan. "I'll ask around."

"If you're able to locate a boat, come on out," said Bryan. "I'll let the deputies know that you're coming so they will let you through."

Jan began to look around the edge of the water to see if there was a boat nearby.

"There's a marina just up the road. Why don't you drive over there and see if they have a rental available?" Bryan suggested.

"That's an idea," she answered.

Joe climbed into the boat, and Bryan pushed away from the shore then scrambled to jump into the front seat as the boat got into deep enough water. After they both were in safely, Bryan lowered the small engine and pulled the crank rope and they slowly pulled away from the landing. Jan watched as they moved around the bend and headed into deeper water. After a few minutes, they arrived back at the recovery site and had to recheck through a couple of county deputies who were trying to keep on-lookers from getting too close. As they were checked in, Bryan talked to the deputy in charge.

"Listen," he began, "there's a lady reporter and her photographer who may be coming out here shortly, if they can find a boat. When you see them, how about letting them through?"

"Sure thing, sir," the deputy answered. "What's the lady's name?"

"Jan Goodson," he answered. "Robert Trent is her photographer. They're from the *Nashville Tennessean*."

Bryan and Joe let their boat idle next to the barge and tied it along the port side of the float. They climbed the rope ladder to the deck and walked up to Sheriff Robinson, who was talking to a man they did not know. As they walked near, Robinson motioned them over and introduced the man to them.

"This is Jack Nelson with the TVA. He has a good knowledge of the lake and the history of the area before the lake was built."

"How do you do, Jack?" asked Joe as he reached out for a handshake. He introduced himself and Bryan, then asked, "Can you give us an idea of the area's geography prior to the construction of the lake?"

"Well, I have a bunch of old geographical survey maps of the area, prior to 1939, when construction began on the lake. This," he said pointing to a spot near center of the map, "is approximately where we are now standing."

"So, according to this map," said Bryan pointing at the map, then motioning with his hand over the lake off the right side of the barge, "we're very near the western end of the town called Rhea Springs. This building here was the church, that's almost directly where we are."

"Well, sir," answered Jack, pointing directly at the site on the map, "by the 40s, or the time that Sheriff Robinson was talking about, all of this was gone and the area had already been excavated."

"So, by mid-1940, there was no one living in this area at all?" asked Bryan.

"The closest houses or business would have been on this side of Toestring Creek between here and the paved road you fellows came in on," answered Nelson, pointing back toward the shore to the west.

"I guess that pretty much rules out the idea that it was somebody local. I think the murder had to take place with someone who was familiar with the construction site and how to get in and out," Joe said to Bryan.

"Still could have been a local," Bryan answered.

"Yep, could be. But I'm thinking more of someone related to the construction of the lake, someone who would know about those forms and how to get to them." Joe turned to the evidence table and noticed that more pieces had been brought up. He began to look at the new artifacts, but saw nothing that was really eye-opening, or relevant to solving the crime.

"I think the key to this thing could be locating some of the people who may have worked on the original project or who were living here at the time," Bryan said.

They turned back to Nelson, and Joe asked, "Do you have a way to get us a list of the people who worked on the project?"

"Sure, I can locate that for you. Might take some time." Nelson looked through the stacks of papers he had brought with him. "Don't have anything here that's related to the employee list. I'll call the Chattanooga office and get them to put it together for us."

"That's great, Jack, give me a call." Joe gave Nelson the information for where he and Bryan were staying, and how to reach them.

"Can you leave us all of this stuff, so we can go through it?" asked Bryan.

"Sure thing, guys. Call me if you have any other questions," he said, offering them each a business card.

"Bryan! Joe!" A familiar voice piped out.

"Looks like your reporter made it out here, Bryan."

They walked over to where their boat was tied and helped Robert and Jan onto the barge.

"You know those two guys from Ohio who found the skull?" asked Jan.

"Yeah, I remember," answered Bryan.

"We gave them twenty-five dollars for the use of their boat."

"Can we photograph any of this stuff?" asked Robert, intently looking at the collection of artifacts on the table.

"Sure thing," answered Bryan, who was obviously smitten by Jan and would do anything to accommodate her. "Shoot anything you want. I'll introduce you around to some of these guys and you can get some details from them also."

"I've never seen you be so helpful to a reporter before," joked Joe, as he elbowed Bryan in the side then smiled at him. "Of course, we haven't worked with many that looked like her either."

Jan and Robert spent the best part of the afternoon taking pictures and talking to the sheriff and his deputies, and the men from the TVA. They were particularly interested in the old maps that Jack Nelson had. They took pictures of him and the sheriff looking at the maps together, as well as putting together a story that tied the history of the area with the murder. After they had finished interviewing and photographing, they informed Joe and Bryan that they were ready to head back to shore to wire the story to the paper for the evening edition. There was a marginal amount of time to make the evening paper, and they both felt an urgency to beat the deadline. As they were getting aboard their boat to leave, Bryan yelled across the barge to Jan. "Don't leave until I talk to you," he said, and began to walk her way.

"Uh-oh!" said Jan in mock concern as she turned to Robert. "What did I do?"

"I can't think of a thing," Robert said, smiling. "I'll wait here for you."

She stepped back aboard the barge and met Bryan halfway across. There were no people but the two of them.

"I didn't want you to leave before I got a chance to ask you out for dinner tonight," he said.

She laughed at his question. "Oh, God. When you yelled out at me, I thought I had done something awful."

Bryan laughed and told her that he did not mean to alarm her. He smiled at her as she nodded her head to affirm his invitation. The smile that came across her face told Bryan that she was pleased with the invitation.

"We're staying at the Holiday Inn in downtown Chattanooga," she added.

"We're at the Admiral Benbow Motel. Why don't you call me when you guys get settled in and we'll decide where you want to go?"

"That's sounds great," she said. "I'll tell Robert to grab something for himself for dinner. You did mean just you and me, didn't you?"

"That's exactly what I had in mind."

She smiled. "I'll call you when we get everything settled in."

Jan was very anxious to get the report filed and the pictures wired to the office as soon as possible, but couldn't wipe off the smile. She also wanted to call her mom in Nashville and tell her all about the big story before it appeared in print. Robert ran the boat at full throttle on the trip back to the campsite and when they got back to the landing, pulled the boat up on shore and thanked the two men for the use of their boat. Robert could sense that Jan was hurrying to get everything packed up and to get on the way.

"We've got to really shake a leg to get this stuff filed," Jan said as they got into the car. "Let's drive straight back to the motel. We can call from there, and you can work on the film while I call this stuff in."

"That sounds like a winner. They've got a photo lab downtown near the motel. That would probably be a quicker way to get the processing done," said Robert. "I can drop this off and wait on it, then we can get together and wire or fax everything in."

"Sure. Why don't you come by my room when you get everything done? We can use the wire services at the *Chattanooga News Free*

Press. It shouldn't take too long," Jan said as she drove through Dayton heading toward Chattanooga.

After they arrived, Robert dropped Jan off in front of the motel and drove on downtown to the photo lab. Jan went into the room and went straight to the phone. Her first call was not to the newspaper, but to her mother. She wanted so much to share this story with her. She also had a desire to share the news of her date with her mother, like she used to years ago. She dialed her mother's number into the motel phone and after a couple of rings heard her mother's voice on the other end. After hellos, Jan told her about the day's events.

"This is probably the biggest story I've ever worked on."

Jan told her about the case, finding the skeleton at the bottom of the lake that had been buried since the lake had been constructed in 1941. She told her about the diver bringing up evidence from the bottom, and about looking through the pieces like putting a giant puzzle together.

"It was so shocking when the fishermen found that skull, but as they began to find more and more, it became exciting," Jan told her mother enthusiastically.

Her mother could sense the writer's enthusiasm in her daughter's voice, and encouraged her to tell her more.

'Then when they found those dog tags and learned the identity— that was even more exciting."

"Who was it?" her mother asked.

"It was a Navy man named Lawrence Gibson, and they think he was from this area."

Her mother didn't respond. There was a rattling sound, and Jan thought her mother had dropped the phone. She called her name with no response. Finally, she heard her mother's shaky breath on the other end of the line.

"Say that name again, dear."

"Lawrence Gibson."

Pause.

"I knew a Lawrence Gibson. Went to school with him. We were…close. Very close…"

"Where did he live?" Jan interrupted.

"Chattanooga. We attended City High School together." From the sound of her voice, Jan could tell that her mother was shaken by the news, but she couldn't pass up the opportunity to get more background on her case. This was a big story for her, and the realization that her mother might have actually known the victim caused her to push harder.

"Maybe you could help give them some information about him. They're going to look into his background on Monday," Jan said. "Do you want me to give them any of this information or pass along your number?"

"No, honey," her mother answered. "I would rather you keep me entirely out of it. I don't really know what happened to Larry after high school. He sort of dropped out of sight."

"All right. I mean, it won't take the FBI long to trace all of that information anyway," said Jan. "Still, I promise not to volunteer the information."

"Do something for me, sweetheart," her mother said as they ended the conversation. "Keep me informed as to what is going on. I'm certain it's the same Larry Gibson that I knew."

"I'll do that, Mom," Jan answered. "I'm sorry if I upset you."

"No, no, dear," her mother answered. "It was a long time ago. It just brought back some memories."

As Kathy hung up the phone, she was shaking uncontrollably. She was trying to figure out in her mind how Larry, who was supposed to be buried in a grave in the Punchbowl National Cemetery in Hawaii, could have been found at the bottom of Watts Bar Lake. This had to have been the reason why Larry did not come home, but who, how, and why were still questions she could not answer. The shaking worsened when she realized that when the FBI traced her whereabouts, Jan would find out the truth about Larry.

Kathy's mind raced back to that day in September of 1949 when she took her husband, Frank, and their daughter to the dedication service of the National Cemetery in the Pu'owaina Crater, known as the Punchbowl, overlooking the city of Honolulu. Supposedly, Larry was among the 776 casualties of Pearl Harbor that were buried there and honored in the opening ceremony to dedicate the site. She had told Jan, who was eight years old at the time, that she was going to the dedication to honor some classmates who had been killed in the attack. Jan and her father had stayed on the beach that day, while Kathy went alone. It would have been too hard to explain it all. As far as Jan knew, Frank Goodson was her father, and she hoped it would always stay that way. She had managed to keep the secret this long, now she could see it slipping away.

As Jan struggled with her mom's reaction, she quickly put it aside and began working on putting the story together. By the time Robert got back with the photos, they were ready to wire the complete story with a couple of the best photos. They got back to the motel a little after six and Robert walked with Jan down the sidewalk toward their rooms. Robert's room was closest, and as he placed his key into the lock, he paused and looked at Jan.

"Well, girl," he began, "it's been a busy day. Where do you want to eat?"

"You're on your own tonight, Robert," she answered, "I've got plans for the evening."

"Ah-ha," he exclaimed, "I knew something was going on with Bryan when we left the barge and he called you back."

"Oh, Robert, you are too perceptive. Nothing gets by you, does it?" she said as she smiled playfully at him and winked.

"When you got back in the boat and didn't say anything, that sort of sealed the deal for me," he answered.

"I hope you don't mind eating alone."

"No, not at all. Maybe I'll get with Joe and we can go somewhere and grab a bite."

Chapter 14
Chattanooga, July 3, 1970

When Jan arrived at her room, she found a note attached to her door. It was in Bryan's handwriting. The note said:

"Sorry I missed you, just dropped by to talk about plans for tonight. I will pick you up at 8, if there's a problem, call me. -Bryan"

She wasn't sure where they were going to eat or what they were going to do, so she decided to dress casually. She showered, changed clothes, and fixed her hair in a French twist. She finally decided on a light blue pant suit and some pale blue flats that she brought along. She didn't really feel dressed up, but it was all that she brought with her that she could think of that was flexible enough for the occasion. It had been a long time since she had been on a date.

It was still thirty minutes until she was expecting Bryan, so she decided to sit in the chair by the window and read. Just as she was settling in, her bedside phone rang.

"Hello," she answered.

"Hey, darling, this is your mother," Kathy's voice came from the other end. "I was sort of worried about how we left the conversation earlier, and I wanted you to know the whole story. Do you have time to talk?"

After talking with her daughter earlier, she had time to evaluate the situation and to come to a decision concerning their relationship with Larry Gibson. It was not fair to her daughter that she keep it from her any longer.

"Sure, Mom," she answered. "I have about thirty minutes before someone is supposed to pick me up. We're going out to eat."

"Oh, you've got a date?" she replied. "That's great. Can't remember the last time you took enough time out to go on a date."

"Well, don't know if you'd call it a date, we just met and we're going out to eat."

"Sounds like a date to me," Kathy teased. She seemed at ease joking with her daughter and it helped her as she moved to the more serious matter she had called about.

"Whatever," Jan rebuffed.

"Listen, I felt like I needed to tell you a little more about Larry, before you find out something and get the wrong idea."

"Sure, Mom. Go ahead." She could sense the more somber tone in her mother's voice and worry came across her face as she turned away from the window to concentrate on what her mother was saying.

"I was very close to Larry in high school. We dated all the way through our senior year, and decided to get married after graduation."

"Wow, that's *really* close," she answered, obviously surprised. "Did you get married?"

"Yes, dear. In 1939. We lived in Chattanooga. He joined the Navy in 1940 and was shipped out to the Pacific in 1941. He was stationed at Pearl Harbor when the Japanese attacked." She was fighting to tell the story without choking up.

"So, he was killed there?"

"Well, that's what I thought." Kathy answered. "Do you remember when you were eight years old and we went to Hawaii on that vacation?"

"Sure, I remember," Jan replied.

"Well, I went to a ceremony at the gravesite by myself while you and your dad stayed on the beach. Do you remember that?"

"I do."

"They were dedicating a new military cemetery for all the sailors, known and unknown, who died at Pearl Harbor that day. Larry's name was among that group."

"So, this person is probably not the same one you married?"

"I'm sure it is." Kathy explained that he was coming home for a short visit while on leave because she had told him of the pregnancy.

She gasped into the phone. "Oh my God, Mom. You're telling me that the person we just discovered at the bottom of the lake could be my dad?"

"I'm telling you that it probably is. He never showed up at the bus station when he was scheduled to come home, and the Department of the Navy says that most of the records related to the time period around the bombing were lost. No one really knows when he left Hawaii, or if he actually left at all. It was just assumed that he was one of the missing."

"This is unbelievable, Mom! I don't know what to say." She held the phone tightly against her ear and she sat speechless with the phone tightly against her ear.

"I'm sorry to hit you with all this now, but I was so afraid that it would come out in the investigation, and I wanted you to hear it from me."

"I've got to really think about all of this. This is a lot to swallow at one time, Mom."

"I know it is sweetheart, and I'm so sorry. I've talked with Frank, and he and I are coming to Chattanooga on Monday. Tell your FBI guy that I will be there to answer any question that he might have. I better let you go, so you can get ready for your date—oops, sorry—dinner outing." Her mom joked lightly, trying to relieve some of the tension created by her revelation."

"Okay, Mom," Jan answered. "Call me again on Sunday night."

"I'll do that. I love you, Jan."

"Love you, too, Mom. Tell Dad hello for me."

She hung up the phone and was totally flustered. She knew that Bryan was due at any time and she needed to get herself together. She went to the bathroom and adjusted her make-up and regained her composure, just as a knock came at the door.

"Just a moment," Jan shouted.

She snapped her compact closed, then opened the door. Bryan was dressed in a pair of khaki slacks and a polo shirt, and looked altogether different from the FBI agent she had left earlier. He looked like the kind of man who wanted to have a good time and forget about work for a while.

Jan grabbed her purse from the bureau and the two of them walked out of the room into the night air. He took her by the arm and led her to his car, the same one they had taken to eat lunch in earlier in the day. She decided that the news she had to share with him could wait until later. She really didn't want anything to spoil her evening with Bryan. It was going to be difficult enough to get through the evening without thinking about all that her mother had told her, but she was going to try her best.

They drove through town and Bryan stopped the car in front of a drive-in restaurant that had carhops who came to the car and took the orders. They had a huge sign on the building in front of where they parked that had the complete menu.

"This is the first drive-in I've been to since high school," Jan said as they waited for a carhop to come take their order.

"Yeah, me, too," said Bryan. "Some of the guys on the job were telling me about this place and I thought it sounded like a neat, informal way to get acquainted."

"Sure, it's great." She turned her attention to the menu. "Wow! What a menu they have, all the old treats I used to just love. Chocolate shakes, corn dogs, cheeseburgers. I don't know what I want." She took his hand and moved closer to him in the front seat and then spoke again. "What are you getting?"

"I think I'll have a cheeseburger with the onion rings, and a chocolate shake," he answered, smiling at her. "That oughta get me going."

"Well, I think I'll have a corn dog, French fries, and a large root beer." She grinned at him. "Maybe we can share."

"I was hoping we could do that." He laughed as other thoughts entered his mind. She smiled and continued the thought.

"I'm sure that we will do a lot of sharing before this night is over," she said as she nudged him in the ribs gently with her elbow.

As the carhop came to the side window, he placed the order with her, and rolled the window back up as she left. The car was air conditioned, so it was more comfortable, as well as more private, with the window up.

"I was thinking that after we ate, we could drive up on Lookout Mountain and walk over to Point Park and look at the lights of the city."

"That sounds great, Bryan. I'd love to do that. I remember going up on Lookout Mountain with my parents when I was in the sixth or seventh grade. I still remember how beautiful it was."

They sat silently, staring at each other as they waited on the food order to arrive, then Bryan broke the silence. "You just seem like your mind is somewhere else right now," he said.

"I really didn't want to get into this, but maybe we should discuss it a little. I just didn't want anything to interfere with our evening,"

"If you'd rather wait, we can," Bryan said. "Whatever you're comfortable with. I certainly didn't want to discuss the case either. Does it concern that?"

"As a matter of fact, it does." Jan squeezed his hand. "I have reason to believe that I might be related to the man whose body we found in the lake."

"Oh, my God, Jan," Bryan said, as a surprised look came upon his face, as he looked over at her.

"I talked to my mother today and told her about the body and gave her the name of the person whose dog tags we found. It's my father, Bryan. My real father."

"You have got to be kidding."

"Mom is coming over here on Monday with my dad, or should I say stepdad, and she said that she would be able to tell you the circumstances." She took his hand in both of hers and looked into his eyes as she continued. "I never even knew I had another father. I always assumed that Frank was my real father, and never had any reason to think otherwise."

The carhop arrived with their food and Bryan rolled his window down to attach the tray, and they immediately began to spread the food out between them. Soon they were munching down on the French fries and onion rings, and sipping on their drinks.

"So, how could this person in the lake be your father? I don't understand," offered Bryan between bites.

She set her fries and corn dog to one side on the seat to explain the circumstances of Larry's disappearance, and how it was assumed that he never returned from Pearl Harbor. She explained that as far as her mother was concerned, her husband was dead and buried in Hawaii. She was born five months later, and her mother moved to Nashville, where she took a job as a receptionist at the insurance company that was run by Frank Goodson. The two of them fell in love, he was willing to adopt Jan as his daughter, and she never knew any different. They had always been the Goodsons, one big beautiful, happy, middle-class family in Nashville.

"That's really all I know about the whole situation," said Jan as she took a bite of her corn dog. "I'm sure my mom can give you all the details, at least what she remembers."

"We'll have time to talk about this later," said Bryan as he put his arm around her and held her to him, "Let's just have a good time tonight."

After they had finished eating, the carhop came back and took their tray, and they drove down Broad Street out of town toward Lookout Mountain. The road up the mountain was steep and curvy, and when they arrived at the top, they saw the markers for Point Park, and he parked the car. They walked through the archway into the park and immediately saw the tall monuments and cannons that were displayed in the park. This was where the famous "Battle Above the Clouds" was fought more than a hundred years earlier. They walked over to the point and sat on a bench overlooking the bend of the

Tennessee River known as Moccasin Bend.

"This is absolutely beautiful, Bryan," she said as she laid her head on his shoulder and snuggled close to him. "I really needed this. Thanks."

"No, thank *you* for coming," he said. As she melted into his arms, he kissed her gently on the lips and looked into her eyes. "This is the most beautiful view I've seen in a while."

"Thank you, Bryan. You are so sweet."

They talked for a few minutes about the case, and Bryan expressed hope that her mother's statement would help to fill in some gaps in the investigation. Bryan told her that when he got back to the motel, he would inform Joe, and they could take a few days off until they had discovered what she could add. He added that Joe had already expressed to him that he would like to be home with his family for the Fourth, if he could.

"I've got a proposition for you, Jan," he said. "A friend of mine who lives in Atlanta offered me some tickets to the Pop Festival over the Fourth. Would you be interested?"

"Oh, Bryan, I would definitely be interested." She looked into his eyes and continued, "That would be the ideal way to get my mind off all this other stuff until Monday."

"That's what I was thinking, too," he said.

"When are we going and how long can we stay?"

"Well, I figure we can leave in the morning, and we'll be staying with my buddy and his wife in Marietta, just north of town. The festival is supposed to be in a little place called Byron, down close to Macon. This is supposed to be Georgia's Woodstock," Bryan said.

"If we're going to do that, we really need to head back, so I can get some stuff together," said Jan. "How early do you want to leave in the morning?"

"I was thinking about five or so," said Bryan. "Traffic into Atlanta was backed up for ninety miles last night with people heading down there."

They walked back to the car and he held the door for her, kissing her gently before closing it. After he got into the car and they began to drive down the mountain, Jan began to talk excitedly about the festival.

"You know, I heard some people at the paper talking about the festival and they were planning to go down there. When I heard them talking, I was dreaming to myself about going," Jan said. "This is just amazing."

"I'm glad you're a rock fan."

"I'm really into Jimi Hendrix, and I love the Allman Brothers Band," she added. "There's supposed to be some rhythm and blues people there, too."

"That's more my style," Bryan chimed in. "I like B.B. King and Jethro Tull. Should be a great festival."

After they arrived at her motel, he walked her to the door, took both her hands and held them, then kissed her gently on the lips. He then told her that he would pick her up at five with a cup of coffee for her.

"That sounds great," she said. "Cream and no sugar. Thanks, Bryan."

He turned and went back toward his car, and she watched as he drove away, thinking about tomorrow. The problems that lay ahead for her could wait until Monday.

The next morning, even leaving at five in the morning didn't solve the problem of the traffic. A trip that normally took two to three hours from Chattanooga to Atlanta took more than five, and that was just to Bryan's friends' house in Marietta. They finally got there at ten thirty and his friends, Gary and Ashley, greeted them.

"Oh, wow, man," Gary said. "I can't believe you came. I had given up on you coming when you called me last night. I came very close to selling the tickets."

"We're glad you didn't." Bryan took Jan's arm and began to introduce her to his friends. "Gary and Ashley Mashburn, I'd like you to meet Jan Goodson. Gary is an agent, too; we went through Quantico together."

"It's so nice to meet you, Jan," said Ashley.

"Thank you for putting up with us and for the tickets. Have you all been down for any of the festival yet?" Jan asked.

"No, we were just planning on going the one day, on the Fourth," Gary answered. "Let me help you with your bags, and Ashley can show you where you are sleeping."

They made their way into the front door and into the foyer of a very nice split-level house. There was a stairway that led downstairs to the basement area, and one that went up to the main level. They followed Gary to the main level, and he led them down the hallway to the last two rooms.

"I had no idea what you guys' sleeping arrangement was," Gary chuckled, then continued, "So I figured I would put Bryan in our son's room right here," pointing to the right. "Jan, you can stay in our room right here," pointing to the left.

"I don't want to put your son out or inconvenience you guys," said Bryan.

"You're not, really. David has gone camping with his best friend, and Ashley and I are going to sleep in the guest room in the basement."

George Hudson

"This looks great," Jan said. "You have a beautiful home."

"Thank you very much," answered Ashley.

After they had deposited their bags into their rooms and freshened up from their drive, Ashley fixed them some sandwiches and chips, and they loaded into their larger family car and took off for the festival. The trip down south of the city to the festival was slow-moving, but they finally arrived. They had to park so far away that the walk into the site took another thirty minutes. It was a sea of people, and the sound of music filled their ears as they entered.

The music was wild and loud, the crowd was young, most of them much younger than they were. The smell of marijuana and the sight of open displays of sex were everywhere. There was not much law enforcement, and drugs were passed openly from hand to hand. It was difficult for Gary, and for Bryan himself to not react as law-enforcement persons. They decided to just ignore what they saw and try to enjoy the music as much as possible.

Wading through the sea of humanity, seeing so many people high or passed out, made the enjoyment of the festival difficult. They got close to the stage where the Allman Brothers were playing, and Jan really got into their music. As Duane Allman played the slide guitar, his brother Greg began to wail out on the vocals:

Don't care how long you go,
I don't care how long you stay,
It's good kind treatment,
Bring you home someday.
Someday baby, you ain't gonna trouble
Poor me, anymore.

Jan remembered the song from an old Muddy Waters' album. She began to sway with the music, and Bryan moved up close to her and

109

they moved their hips together in rhythm to the beat.

As darkness began to descend on the festival, the stages lit up with more lights and more performers. After they had heard the Jimi Hendrix performance, they decided to head on back to the car. It had been an eventful day, and one that truly had gotten Jan's mind off the idea that her father had been lying at the bottom of a lake for almost thirty years. That was something she was going to have to face soon enough. The lyrics to the last Jimi Hendrix song kept washing through her mind:

Purple haze, all in my eyes,
Don't know if it's day or night.
You got me blowing, blowing my mind.
Is it tomorrow, or just the end of time?

There was a lot for Jan to think about on the drive back to Marietta.

Like that other southern belle from Atlanta in days gone by, she'd worry about that tomorrow.

The next morning, after a nice breakfast and a little friendly time with Gary and Ashley, they prepared for their trip back to Chattanooga. They loaded the bags into the trunk of Bryan's car, climbed into the seat and waved goodbye as they drove north out of town. The trip back was much less time-consuming and they arrived in Chattanooga after three hours. It had been a nice trip for Jan, a good diversion to take her mind off things for a while. Bryan had been a perfect gentleman, and aside from the closeness and an occasional kiss, there had been no sexual advances toward her at all. She was relieved that it had not happened, but at the same time, felt that it might soon. She really liked Bryan and she knew that he felt the same way toward her. It was just a matter of time. As they brought the bag back into her motel room, Bryan closed the door behind him and set the suitcase on the rack at the end of the bed.

"I had a great time with you at the festival," he said as he took her by the hand.

"I did, too, Bryan. I enjoyed meeting your friends. They were very sweet."

"The pop festival had a little more pop than I thought it would. I was talking with one of the deputies there, and he said the size of the thing caught them by complete surprise. There were only a handful of local guys to keep the order. No way to control all that was going on there." Bryan sat down in the chair next to the bed.

"Looked like a bunch of kids letting off a lot of steam," Jan said. "I didn't see many people our age or older."

Bryan's demeanor seemed to change as his mind went back to the unfinished conversation with Jan about the body in the lake. The FBI investigator in him seemed to emerge from within him as he sat there.

"Why don't we take a little time to rest up, and maybe we can meet again for supper. I would really like to finish our conversation about what you mother said."

"That's a good idea," she answered. "I told her I would be back this afternoon and she promised she would call me about when they were coming in tomorrow."

"Okay, let's see, it's eleven o'clock now," he said. "Why don't I call you about four, and we can meet then?"

It was a little after four when Jan's phone rang and she assumed it was Bryan. She was surprised to hear her mother's voice instead of Bryan's on the other end of the phone. She told her that they would be coming in on a flight from Nashville in a company plane that was due to arrive at ten. She told her that they had made arrangements to rent a car and that they had a room booked at the Read House Hotel, downtown. She also told her that they would get together after Jan got in from work and they could discuss things then.

"Beth was a good friend during that time, too, so she's going to take the day off tomorrow and we are going to catch up on things and try to figure all this out." Her mom sounded exasperated.

"That sounds good, Mom," Jan said. "I told Bryan about our conversation and he told me to tell you that we could all get together later and talk about what you remember."

"Okay, sweetheart," Kathy said. "See you tomorrow afternoon."

"Goodbye, Mom," Jan said. "Have a good trip."

After she hung up the phone, she called Bryan. She reminded him that her mom was coming in tomorrow morning and that Kathy was anxious to talk with him about what she could remember.

"Why don't you come over here in about an hour?" Jan began. "You can bring a few burgers and fries and a couple of cokes and we can eat here and talk about the case. I don't really feel like going out anywhere tonight. Just wanna go to bed early, it's been a long day."

"That sounds good to me, Jan."

Jan took a long shower and changed into a pair of capris and a sleeveless white blouse. She felt more at ease and ready to talk to Bryan about the life she didn't remember. After she sat in the chair to read the morning paper, Bryan knocked on the door.

"Anybody home in there?" he said through the door.

"It depends on who it is and what they have."

She looked through the peephole of the door and Bryan reacted by holding the bag of burgers in front of it and then smiling at her as she peeped through.

"Well, it's the big bad wolf, and I'm bearing burgers and fries," he answered.

She opened the door and greeted Bryan, who had two large bags of food and a cardboard cup carrier, with two drinks.

"You ever had any Krystals?"

"You betcha. They are one of my favorite things."

"Well, I've got a dozen of them here and plenty of fries, so eat hardy."

They spread the food and drinks out on the dresser in the room and sat on the edge of the bed with their food and began to eat. Jan had not eaten since breakfast, so the small Krystal burgers went down fast with the fries and Coke.

"That was really good, thanks," she said as she wiped her mouth with a napkin.

"You're welcome," he answered. "I'm glad you enjoyed them."

As she cleaned up, she began to talk about what she knew.

"All I really know about the situation is what my mother told me the other day on the phone," she began. "Like I said before, there was no mention of my real dad ever."

"But your mom said that they lived in Chattanooga."

"That's what she said."

"And she did say that he joined the Navy a month or so before Pearl Harbor."

"When she took me to Hawaii when I was eight years old, that was the only real connection I have to him. I really didn't know at the time what was going on, or why she went there."

"So, there's not really much more that you know?"

"She said that my dad was supposed to come home on leave from Hawaii and that he never showed up, so they all assumed that he was one of the casualties there. My mom and her friend Beth are going to get together tomorrow and they are going to try and put some pieces together."

"What do you know about Beth?" he asked. "Have you ever met her?"

"I know that she was my mom's friend from the past. She's been to our house in Nashville a couple of times to visit, but I really know nothing about her."

"Why don't we go for a drive?" Bryan suggested. "It'll do us good to get some fresh air."

"That's a great idea," added Jan. "There's a great Civil War battlefield about thirty minutes from here."

"Are you some kind of a history buff?"

"I studied history in college, and got really interested in the Civil War," she answered.

She had talked about her dad at the bottom of the lake as much as she could, and she knew that her mom could help Bryan more than she, so the trip to the Chickamauga Battlefield would be a good diversion for her right now.

"Sounds good. Let's go," agreed Bryan, taking her hand and leading her out the door.

Chapter 15
Chattanooga, July 5, 1970

As they drove up to the battlefield, Jan began to spurt out fact after fact about the battle. It seemed obvious to Bryan that Jan needed to talk about something besides the case, so he listened intently to her presentation. They had stopped at the visitors' center to get a brochure with a route for the driving tour. As they drove, she told him that there were three of four major battles fought within twenty miles of this site. Following the battle at Chickamauga, there were battles at Lookout Mountain, Missionary Ridge, and another battle in Chattanooga.

"The battle that was fought here was, by far, the bloodiest of all of them," she said. "It was really the last major victory for the South."

It took them about an hour to drive the route and by the end of the drive the sun was beginning to set over the ridge behind them. Bryan stopped the car at the parking lot near the Wilder Tower and they walked over to a couple of benches close to the tower in order to be in the shade.

"Tell me about you, Bryan," Jan started. "How did you get involved with doing this kind of work?"

"Well," he began, "like most, I started out wanting to do something else and I ended up here."

"What did you want to do?"

"I had my mind set on being a high school football coach."

"That's exactly where I would have guessed you started." She looked at him and chuckled. "So what pulled you away from that?"

"After I did my student teaching, I began to really become concerned about kids living in an environment that encouraged them into a life of crime."

"You taught at an inner city school?"

"Yeah, right outside D.C.," he continued, "so I made up my mind to go into law enforcement."

"That's quite a leap. So you changed your major?"

"No. Actually, I went ahead and graduated with a teaching degree, but ended up with a job in law enforcement."

"Where did you work?"

"I started out working in a small county sheriff's office in Northern Virginia. My boss was a great motivator, and he kept pushing me in the right direction. I ended up taking the exam and got accepted by the FBI and was sent to Quantico for training. Been with them now for ten years."

"So that's where you met Gary?"

"Yeah, we met there. Gary ended up in the Atlanta office, and I worked out of Memphis," he explained, as they sat on the bench in front of the cannons overlooking the battle site.

Jan took Bryan's hand in hers and pointed with the other at the horizon and the setting sun. "Isn't that beautiful?"

"Not as beautiful as the person whose hand I'm holding," he said, moving his face closer to hers and kissing her softly on the lips.

"Thank you," she whispered, and returned his kiss.

Afterwards, they walked hand in hand down the shaded road toward the tower, where they continued conversing.

"What about Jan Goodson?" he asked. "How is it she ended up at this place and time in this job?'

"I went to a large public high school in Nashville, played basketball," she answered. "I wanted to go into law or medicine."

"Basketball?" He stopped, turned, and looked her in the eyes. "I had you pegged for a cheerleader, or something more laid back. Band, maybe."

"I wasn't very good. I only played because my best friend played."

"So what else did you do in high school?"

"I was in several clubs and organizations and worked on the school newspaper for three years and was editor my senior year. That's where I became interested in writing and working for a newspaper."

They continued to walk, holding hands, and occasionally shielding the setting sun from their eyes as it peered through the trees.

"So where to from there?" continued Bryan.

"I was lucky enough to get a full scholarship in journalism at the University of Tennessee," Jan added.

"How was college life for you?"

"Not very good," she added. "I had a hard time adjusting to college life and being away from home. I met this guy..." She stopped suddenly and picked up a couple of stones and began to throw them in the woods beside the trail.

"Uh, oh, bet I know the rest of this story," he said as he stopped walking and faced her as she talked.

"We lived together through a year of hell, determined to finish my degree. In spite of everything I went through that year, I kept my grades high enough to retain my scholarship."

"Must have been a real struggle for you."

"It was. I never would have made it if my mom and dad had not stood by me and supported me. It was really tough."

Jan went on to tell Bryan that her parents were always honest with her, and that she had never had any reason to doubt anything they ever told her. She knew that she looked an awful lot like her mother and not at all like her father, but that didn't seem to bother her that much. She recounted how the three of them were always doing things as a family, Frank and Kathy always spending as much time as they could with her.

"That's one of the reasons I'm having such a difficult time with all this," she confessed. "It's just so hard to believe."

"Are you going to continue working on the story?" he asked.

"If my editor will let me, I want to," she said. "It will give me an entirely new slant on the story, but it should be very interesting to do."

The trail formed a loop at the top of a hill and they were circling back toward the parking lot beside the tower. The shadows on the road were getting longer as the sun was disappearing behind the ridge to the west.

"One of the great things about this assignment was meeting you," he said, as he looked into her eyes.

"I feel the same way, Bryan," she said. "I'm just so distracted right now with all this other stuff. Forgive me, if I'm not totally into this dating thing right now."

"No, no. I understand completely. Things will work out,"

He walked her back to the car and they drove back through town toward the motel. On the way back through town they stopped at an ice cream shop called Kay's Kastle that had a huge ice cream cone for a sign. They got their cones and sat down at a small table on two metal chairs to eat and talk a little more about the case. Bryan told her that

Joe was due back later that night and that he would fill him in on all that had happened since he left. By the end of the night, it seemed obvious that there were a lot of pieces missing to the puzzle.

Purple Haze

Chapter 16
Crime Scene, July 6, 1970

On the way to the dive site, Bryan filled in the details for Joe concerning the identity of the body. Like Bryan, Joe had a difficult time reconciling the story and trying to determine why Jan's dad ended up at the bottom of the lake in a construction form. They took their boat out to the dive site and saw that more and more of the pieces had been found and that there was now an almost complete skeleton. The skull had been returned by the Hamilton County forensic people and it now lay appropriately at head the skeletal body. Most all of what remained of the uniform and clothing were neatly arranged and were being tagged by the forensic people, in preparation for shipping back to the lab for closer identification.

The divers had successfully disassembled the construction form using underwater cutting equipment and tools. The form had remained unmoved since the lake had been made and about one-half of it remained buried under river silt and had to be dug out. There was no hope of recovering any fingerprints from any of the evidence since it had been exposed to water for such a long period of time. There were several pieces that were recovered from around the form during the excavation, but it was difficult to tell if they had been there at the time of the burial or had washed up later. Among those pieces was an old

Case pocket knife that had one of the blades broken off, which could have been there at the beginning, since it was discovered at the base of the form under two feet of accumulated silt and rock.

The sheriff walked up to the pair as they were looking over the new artifacts. "Looks like we're about to wrap it up here. The divers have done all they can do, and I think we've gotten about all we're gonna get from down there."

"So, what's the next step for you guys?" Joe asked Sheriff Robinson.

"We're going to have to see if we can figure out exactly who this feller was and how he ended up in Rhea County."

Bryan filled in the sheriff about the identity of the body and told him that the investigation was now centered around Chattanooga and the surrounding area.

"I suspect," Bryan began, "that the crime was committed in Hamilton County and that this was the dump site because the person who committed the crime knew when the lake was going to be filled and how to access the site."

"That would have been thirty years ago or more," the sheriff said. "That's going to take a lot of work to uncover a crime that old, that the person got away with for so long."

"Well, we've got a big piece of the puzzle already solved," Joe said. "We'll dig up some more stuff in the next few days."

Jan and Robert had decided to stay away from the site and to do their story as the pieces were solved. They had enough pictures of the dive site, and the real story now lay in the past and the uncovering of the crime itself. She had told Robert that he was free to go back home and that she could rent a car and stay in Chattanooga. Jan had also called her boss at the paper and she had been given the go-ahead to work the story on her own for a few days. She waited for Bryan and Joe, but they did not return as soon as she had hoped, so she and Robert took off for the Chattanooga airport so she could rent a car and Robert could head on back to Nashville. It was getting close to time for her parents to land so she decided to go into the airport and get a snack while she waited for them. Kathy and Frank landed on time in Chattanooga in a plane owned by Frank's insurance company, and Jan greeted them at the arrival gate. They picked up a rental car; Jan followed them downtown to the Read House hotel. After her parents had checked in, she informed them she was going back to her motel to take a shower, and that she would be back in a short while. They all hugged. After settling into their room, Kathy called Beth to find out where Beth and she could meet.

"How are you feeling, Beth?" Kathy asked her.

Beth told her that she had been in good health and had been doing great. She expressed her shock about the discovery and told her friend that she was available to help her with filling in some unknown details. They both agreed that after thirty years, things were going to be difficult to remember. She took the handheld phone and walked over to the window, just in time to see Jan drive out of the parking lot.

"Have you heard anything yet about the recovery?" asked Beth.

"Just what has been on the news the last couple of days. Not much has come out yet." Kathy replied, exasperation obvious in her voice.

"Do you have time to meet, dear?" Beth asked her. "There's a coffee shop downstairs at the Read House. Why don't we meet there? Then we can head over to the public library; I thought it might be good to look through some old newspapers from back then and do a little research on the time period that it all happened," Beth answered.

"Sounds good. What time?"

"Give me about thirty minutes."

"Why don't you just come by my room and we can leave from here?"

"All right. See you then, Kathy."

"Bye."

After she hung up the phone, she talked with Frank about their plans. He told her not to worry about him because he was going over to the Chattanooga office of their company to talk with some of the agents there. He told her that he would probably be back around two or three in the afternoon.

"Beth and I will just grab some lunch on the run," she said.

"Are you going to call Jan?" he asked.

"I'll probably try later," she answered. "She said she would get back with us after she showered."

"I may try to call her from the office and see if she is there," Frank said as he looked at his watch. "Maybe she and I can have lunch together."

"I think that would be perfect," she said. "Why don't you call her room at the Holiday Inn and plan it with her?"

She turned her back to Frank and began walking toward the bathroom, kicking off her shoes on the way. "I'm going to take a shower and change into something more comfortable before Beth gets here."

When Beth knocked on the door, Frank was looking in the mirror, tying his tie. He grabbed his jacket and slipped it on just as Kathy opened the door.

"Beth! It's good to see you again," he said whlile Kathy and Beth embraced in the doorway. "I'm sorry the conditions aren't more ideal."

"Yeah, it's difficult, I'm sure," she answered as she squeezed Kathy's hand.

"It's going to be tough to remember back thirty years," Kathy said. "Where does one start?"

"Well, for now, let's just talk. We might remember some things in the process if we put our heads together," said Beth.

"You ladies have good luck with your search. I'll see you later, Beth, and we can all have supper together," said Frank as he was leaving the room.

"That sounds great. I'm looking forward to it," answered Beth as he walked out the door.

After Frank got to the offices on Market Street, he used the phone in the conference room and called the motel where Jan was staying. After the third ring, Jan answered. She told him that she was ready to go and that she could get together with him whenever he was available. They decided to meet at Shoney's restaurant just off Tenth Street for lunch at twelve thirty. Frank explained that he wanted to make some contacts with some of his people while he was there and that he would be finished by then and they would have plenty of time to talk.

Jan was interested in looking at the old newspaper articles from 1941, to see if she could find any clues as to what happened with her biological father. After she hung up the phone with her dad, she got in her car and drove down to the public library. When she got there she went to the reference area and asked to see microfiche copies of the New York *Times*, the Chattanooga *Times,* and the Chicago *Sun-Times*, that covered the time period of November and December of 1941. After she got the canisters of film, she went into the projection room and began looking through them in order by day.

There was no mention of anything that was related to the events in early December or to her dad's name at all, until she found the mention of his name along with a dozen or so other names of people from the East Tennessee area that were officially missing at Pearl Harbor. That paper was dated December 21, 1941, so it had taken about two weeks for the Navy to publicly announce that he was missing. The only other mention of Larry Gibson appeared in an article dated December 10, 1941, and it was concerning his mother, or the person who would have been her grandmother.

The body of Louise Gibson was discovered by a neighbor yesterday, after the neighbor said that she was returning a borrowed dish. The neighbor became concerned when she had not seen Mrs. Gibson around the house for a couple of days and discovered a torn front screen door. Police are still investigating the murder, and no suspects have been named. It seems that Mrs. Gibson was killed with a kitchen knife when she apparently surprised a burglar. She is survived by her son Lawrence, who is presently serving in the U.S. Navy.

She decided to make a copy of the article, and possibly do some checking on the case later with the police department to see if anyone was ever arrested or what became of the case file. She looked at her watch and it was already twelve ten, she would have just enough time to check the stuff back in, get her copy, and meet her dad for lunch at twelve thirty. She at least had some things to check out after lunch.

When she arrived at Shoney's, she saw her dad sitting on the front bench outside the restaurant. The two of them embraced and then walked inside and were seated in a booth near the center of the restaurant.

"It's good to see you, Dad," she began. "How was Mom this morning?"

"It's good to see you, too," Frank answered with a smile. "Your mom seemed to be okay when she left with Beth this morning. She's shaken by all this."

After the waitress took their order, they continued to catch each other up with what was going on in their lives. Jan told him about the rock festival and about all she saw going on there. He told her about how his insurance business was doing, and then they talked about what he could remember about meeting her mom and starting the family together.

"When your mom came to work with me, she really didn't have much experience, but she had a great personality and terrific smile that I thought I could use in the front office," he said. "So I put her in the front as a receptionist."

"Just answering phones and greeting people, huh?"

"Yeah," he answered. "She really wanted to do more so she went to classes at night to learn more secretarial skills and began to move up in the organization." He paused for a moment when the waitress brought their food, and then continued. "I had lost my first wife to cancer three years earlier, and didn't think I would ever marry again. Until I met Kathy."

"Did you know she had a daughter?"

"Sure," he answered. "She brought you to work several times when she had babysitter problems. I fell in love with you, too."

"What did you know about her previous life and about Larry?"

"I knew that she had a difficult time after she lost him. She told me about the two of you moving to Nashville with nothing but your clothes, and living with a friend of hers. She worked for a while at a Woolworth's downtown, and then she said she worked at a laundry."

"She really had a hard time readjusting, then?"

"She did," he answered. "I remember when she came to work here, she seemed so excited about working in an office. It was new for her, and she really took to it well."

"How long did she work for you before you two were married?"

"She had been here for about a year when we started dating. Let's see," he said, trying to remember the exact time frame. "That was '44, I think. I asked her to go to a church social with me, and we continued dating after that."

Frank told her about the problems that Kathy had encountered as a single mother, trying to support herself an a daughter. After she married Frank, she quit her job and became a full-time housewife. He said that her mom always had good things to say about Larry and never had any regrets except that he was killed in the war. They talked about the trip to Hawaii (which was paid for by the Navy) and the finality of officially burying Larry.

"After we returned to the States," he said, "she was determined to start anew and had a better outlook on life."

"Still, it must have been difficult for you."

"It was," he answered, "but it was much harder on her. I'm just glad that I was here for her, to help her through it."

After they sat there for ten or fifteen more minutes and discussed early life as a family, they said their goodbyes, and Jan returned to her research work at the library and Frank returned to the office downtown to talk with his employees. It had been a good meeting for Jan, and she had been made more aware of the difficult times that her mom had after her dad was gone.

Kathy and Beth drove through the old neighborhood and discovered that their houses were still standing but the neighborhood itself was rundown. Most of the houses had not been painted in a while and very little in the way of renovation had been done on any of it. They looked at the names on the mailboxes but didn't see any they could recall from the "old days." The store on the corner, where Kathy used to walk to get groceries every now and then, was now a liquor store. Most of the kids in the neighborhood seemed to be lower class and there was a mixture of races in the once all-white neighborhood.

As they were about to become discouraged, they passed a familiar house at the end of the street where Beth had once lived. The name on the mailbox was Hutchinson. As they slowed past the box, Beth suddenly recalled the name.

"You remember the Hutchinsons?" Beth asked Kathy. "Mr. Hutchinson used to always fuss at us about making too much noise at night in front of his house."

"Oh, yeah, I remember," Kathy said. "He worked late at night and slept in the daytime. He hated being woken up during the day."

"Mrs. Hutchinson would always apologize after he yelled at us. She'd ask us in and have something good to feed us."

"Oh, yeah, the woman with the pecan pies," Kathy said. "I used to love those pies she made. She wrote out the recipe for me once, but I couldn't cook a lick, and they always turned out bad."

They stopped the car in front of her house and the two of them walked up the walkway to the front door. After a few knocks, a shadow appeared in the sheer curtain that was lining the front door, and the door opened. An old woman with a big smile came to the door and the two of them recognized her immediately.

"Mrs. Hutchinson?" Kathy began. "We used to come over here and eat pecan pie with you years ago. Do you remember us?"

"No," she answered. "I can't rightly say that I do. My mind slips on me every now and then."

"We used to walk in front of your house years ago," Beth said, "and purposely make noise so your husband would yell at us."

"Well, Walter yelled at everybody," she said. "Hmm, I might remember you two, though. Seems like both of you had husbands in the war if I recollect."

"That's right," they answered. "Your mind is still sharp."

"Well, come on in," she said. "Can't say that I've got any pecan pie, but I'll be glad to fix you ladies some tea."

After they sat in the parlor, Mrs. Hutchinson went into the kitchen and they sat looking at pictures of her husband and familiar photos of what she looked like in 1941. After she returned with the tray and the cups of tea, the three of them sat and talked about the neighborhood. The only recollection that she could give to them about the time period after Kathy had moved away and sold the house, was a fellow in a black pickup truck who kept driving through the neighborhood really slow past her old house.

"Yeah," Mrs. Hutchinson said, "it was really strange. That went on for three or four months, almost every evening after you moved out. I wrote down the license plate number and gave it to a policeman in the neighborhood, but I reckon nothing ever came of it."

"Did you ever see the driver?" Kathy asked.

"No," she responded. "Never did see him, he just drove through and never stopped. But he always drove really slow past your house."

Kathy and Beth looked at each other and realized who she was speaking of. Neither of them had any doubt as to who this person was.

Both began to rise and place their teacups back on the tray and thanked Mrs. Hutchinson for her time.

"It was so nice to see you again," Kathy said as she stood up.

"It was good to see you too, my dear. Don't have many visitors anymore. Most of the neighbors have moved away or passed on."

"Thanks for your help, Mrs. Hutchinson," said Beth as they walked to the door and back to their car.

"That was certainly enlightening," said Kathy. "I always thought that Dan could be capable of something like this. He really had me scared when I moved away. He was very possessive."

They drove back through town and stopped in front of the public library. They parked their car and went into the building and were directed to an area where old newspaper articles were filed. When they entered, they were surprised to see Jan sitting at one of the viewers looking at old articles. Kathy walked up behind her and put her hand on her shoulder and called her name. Jan immediately stood and the two of them embraced. She told them what she had found so far and shared with them where she had looked and what she had looked for.

"I called my editor," Jan said, "and told him that this case involved my family and that I wanted to take a little time to pursue some leads."

"So, you've taken a leave or some time off?" asked Kathy.

"No, I'm still working this story, but from a different angle."

"We're working on something, too," said Kathy. "We'll say goodbye before we leave. You go on ahead with what you were doing."

Jan was curious about what her mother had found, but she knew she would have time later to question her about it. She was also anxious to keep digging in the old newspapers.

"Sure, Mom. Good luck."

After spending an hour in the files and looking through old articles, they found very little of any help concerning Dan and what became of him after she left town in '42. She said goodbye again to Jan and told her that they would get together later that afternoon and to call her at the hotel when she finished.

There was still a chance that they might find some clues by contacting some of Dan's old friends. The only name that Kathy could recall was Sam Daniels, who rode with Dan to the Watts Bar job every day. She had never met him personally, but she remembered Dan talking about him often. It wasn't much, but at least it was a start. She looked through a phone book that covered the area and saw three people with that name, so she wrote down the numbers and began calling them.

Chapter 17
Chattanooga, July 8, 1970

The second Sam Daniels that Kathy called turned out to be the one who worked with Dan on the TVA project. He agreed to meet her and Beth at the Eastgate Mall in front of J.C. Penney's at three. They parked as close as possible to the entrance of the store and walked through the men's department, through the jewelry department and out the mall entrance, and saw Sam sitting on the bench in front of the store. He was a heavy man of better than three hundred pounds, medium height, with a full grey beard that matched his long hair. He looked exactly as he had described himself to her on the phone. As they walked over to him, he rose and reached out his hand to greet them.

They exchanged greetings and began to talk about Sam's knowledge of Dan and what became of him. He told them that after the Watts Bar project, the two of them worked for a while on the Hales' Bar project and then decided to join the Army. He said that they agreed to enlist together so they would be sent out together. The two of them trained at Parris Island in South Carolina and were shipped out to North Africa, fighting in the same battalion throughout the war.

"The thing I remember the most about Dan," recalled Sam, "was how he constantly talked about you. Last thing he said to me when we shipped home was that he was going to find you and start a life together with you."

"It was a one-way infatuation," Kathy said. "When I lived here before the war, I spent the last few months in Chattanooga, dodging him."

"I had no idea," Sam confessed. "From everything he told me, you two were madly in love and once you were free, his life was set."

"Do you remember anything specifically about the first few weeks of December, 1941?" Beth said, entering the conversation.

"Yes, ma'am," he responded. "That was when we finished the Watts Bar job and they filled the lake. Remember that week well."

"Why is that?" Kathy asked.

Sam's face was flushed and he began to squirm around on the bench.

"That was a long time ago, ma'am," he answered. "Can't say that I recall anything specifically he said, but I do remember him being upset about Larry coming home."

Both Kathy and Beth could sense that Sam was growing uncomfortable with the questions and Kathy decided to hone in on that uneasiness.

"Do you know where Dan is now?" asked Kathy bluntly.

Sam told them that they had kept in touch pretty closely though the years and that Dan was living in South Florida. He told her that Dan and his brother operated a company that salvaged old ships off the coast there. He said that they get together every couple of years with some of his other army buddies in various places. The last time they had gotten together, Dan invited all of them to go deep sea fishing. That was in the late spring of 1967. That was the last time that he had seen Dan.

They thanked him for his time and he exited the mall, through the side entrance to the mall rather than the way they had entered. They sat at the metal table together and watched him walk through the exit doors and discussed what Sam's revelations could mean. They were already aware that Dan worked on the Watts Bar project when it was being built. This fact combined with what Sam had told him about Dan's jealousy, helped the pieces fall into place. They exited the mall and headed back to the rental car to drive back to the Read House and contemplate their next move. They were really no closer to finding the answer than they were when they started. Kathy had a strong feeling that the answer would be related to Dan. There was a piece there that she could not put her finger on, but she just felt he was involved.

After the ladies had left the mall, Sam exited his pickup truck and reentered the mall, walking over to pay phones in the center of the mall. He dug through his wallet and found the number he needed, inserted the coins and dialed the number.

On the third ring, a voice came on the line. "Bowers' Salvage," Dan said into the phone.

"Hey, buddy," answered Sam. "You need to call me back at this number, so we can talk. Got a little problem here, but I'm on a pay phone and don't have much change." He gave him the number and hung the phone up. In a few minutes, the pay phone rang, and Sam answered it.

"What's the problem, Sam?" asked Dan.

"Just got through talking to your old girlfriend, Kathy," Sam replied.

"Man, hadn't thought about Kathy in years. How's she doing?"

"Not too good, man," answered Sam. "They just found a body under the lake up here at Watts Bar, and they've identified it as her husband."

"What?" Dan leaned back in his chair and looked out the window at the dock that extended into the deeper water and rubbed his free hand on his temple at a suddenly appearing headache. "I thought he had been killed in the war."

"You and I both know that ain't true, man. You better get your ass up here and help me figure this thing out. It's just a matter of time before they pull me in on this. They got the FBI up here nosing around."

"Okay, Sam, look," answered Dan, "I'll get a flight up to Chattanooga as soon as I can get away. You still got the same number at home?"

"Yeah, man," Sam replied, "Give me a call when you get into town and I'll come and pick you up."

"No, I don't think that would be a good idea," answered Dan. "I'll rent a car and get a motel room and then call you so we can meet."

Sam was extremely nervous after the phone call, and decided that the best thing he could do would be to lay low for a few days, meet with Dan and stay out of sight. It was only a matter of time until they would knock on his door and he would be dragged into this mess.

Sam's recollection of the events of that week was still fresh in his mind, particularly after Larry's disappearance. Dan had paid him a hundred dollars to wait for the bus that was coming in at 11 p.m. He knew that he could use the money, and the job seemed easy enough. Dan had told him to meet Larry and give him a ride. He was instructed to bring him to the Sky Harbor Courts on South Broad Street and Dan would meet him there with the money. If Larry asked any questions, which Dan was sure Larry would, he was to tell Larry that his wife Kathy had been taken to the hospital with complications, and his buddy Dan was waiting for him at a motel where he was staying. Dan was sure that if he stayed out of sight and wasn't seen with Larry, that it would help cover his tracks. The motel was far enough out of town, that it would provide a safe harbor for him at the time. Sam was to tell him that Dan and Phyllis had gotten a divorce and that he was staying at the motel until he found a place to live

He saw the bus pull into the station and watched as the passengers began to disembark. He wasn't really sure what Larry looked like, although Dan had given him a description. It made it much easier to pick him out, when only two men in military uniforms got off the bus, one in the familiar Army green and the other in Navy white. He yelled out Larry's name, and the young man in the white uniform waved and began to move his way.

As Larry moved closer, Sam reached out his hand and introduced himself. "Hey Larry, I'm Sam Daniels. I work with Dan and he sent me down here to meet you."

"Where's Kathy?" he asked, as he searched the bus station for his wife.

"That's why I'm here, Larry," he began. "Kathy was taken to the hospital today for something minor and couldn't meet you here."

"What about Dan, where is he?" he asked, with a puzzled look on his face.

"He's having some problems of his own. His wife threw him out of the house yesterday, and he's staying over at the Sky Harbor Courts over on south Broad Street. Been going through some rough times and wasn't feeling up to meeting you here tonight. That's why he sent me over here," Sam explained.

"So, are you taking me home?" Larry asked.

"No. Dan asked me to bring you to the motel. You can sleep there tonight, then the two of you can go and see Kathy tomorrow morning." As Sam finished his explanation, he reached for some of Larry's luggage. "Let me take some of those bags. I'm parked right over this way."

The two men drove in relative silence during the short drive over to the motel. When they entered the motel lot, Larry saw Dan, who waved at them. They parked and Larry got out of the car and ran over to Dan, who met him with a huge hug and patted him on the back.

"Man, it's good to see a familiar face," Larry said.

"Yeah. Sorry I wasn't there to pick you up."

"Yeah, that's too bad, Dan. Sam told me about your problems."

"Let's get these bags in the room; I've got special permission to take you up to the hospital to see Kathy, just as soon as you get here."

"That's great, I'm really looking forward to seeing her, thought I was gonna have to wait until morning. You sure it's okay, this time of night?"

"Yeah, I've got it worked out. One of the orderlies is gonna meet us at the emergency entrance and walk us up to the room."

Dan turned to Sam and put his hand on his shoulder. "Thanks for helping me out, man. I'll see you again on Monday morning." As they were talking, Dan handed Sam an envelope and they said their final goodbyes. He had a very uneasy feeling about that night, but even now, he felt the less he knew at the time, the better.

Chapter 18

Signal Mountain Highway, July 9, 1970

It was a gruesome sight. The black pickup truck had plowed through the guard rail on the S-curve coming down Signal Mountain and careened straight down for 1,500 feet. The only thing that prevented its smashing into the valley floor below was a huge oak tree that stopped the falling vehicle halfway down. The wrecker company had spent the better part of the morning winching the demolished truck back up the ravine to the roadside. The Hamilton County Sheriff's Department had contacted Joe Mallory earlier that morning: The person driving the truck was a person of interest in the case over at Watts Bar. The name Sam Daniels had come up.

Joe and Bryan arrived on the site about an hour later. The identity of the driver had already been established. His name was Sam Daniels.

Joe and Bryan used their IDs and were routed around the line of traffic that had backed up for miles going up the mountain. Once in sight of the numerous flashing lights, they were directed through the police barrier. They ended up walking the last 100 yards numerous officers and the work crew.

According to the officers from the county and from the Tennessee Highway Patrol, it was a one-vehicle crash and had happened around 6 a.m. There were no witnesses to the actual crash. A vehicle going up the mountain sometime after it happened saw the demolished guard rail, stopped, looked down and saw the aftermath. He drove on to the first house he came to, more than half a mile away. Because of the delay in reporting, the county did not arrive on the scene for more than an hour more. By the time they got to the car, it was clear that there was no chance of reviving victim. The first medic to arrive on the scene pronounced the unlucky occupant dead on impact. As there was no gasoline leakage or fire, the body was extracted and removed before they began to worry about how to get the truck out of the tree.

Joe and Bryan looked down at the body that lay on the gurney being loaded into the waiting ambulance. There was very little chance that Sam had lived long after he had crashed through the rail. The Highway Patrol officer had told them that the truck was traveling more than 70 miles per hour when he actually left the highway. Preliminary reports suggested there had been a mechanical failure, probably brakes. From the position of the driver it was possible he had passed out before impact. They would know more after they did the autopsy and looked more carefully at the truck.

"I got a call last night from Jan," Bryan said to Joe. "She told me that her mother had been talking to some of the people who they knew from the 1940s. She spoke with this guy just the other day."

"That's quite a coincidence, Bryan."

"I'm supposed to talk with Jan this afternoon," answered Bryan. "But given all this, maybe I should do that as soon as possible. We might be able to find out more about this man and how he fits in to all this."

"You think Jan's mother could be in danger?" Joe asked.

"Could be," Bryan answered. "Better get the sheriff's people to notify her and let her know that she needs to stay at the hotel until we meet with her."

"Good idea," Joe said. "Somebody out there has secrets they obviously don't want anyone to find out."

"I'll contact our lab people and have them send over a crew to go over the truck with a fine-tooth comb. Let's see what they find. Good thing there was no fire. A lucky break, I guess." Bryan looked back at the body, and then to Joe. "See if you can find out his address. We can search his residence and see what's there—might find a clue."

"Good idea," said Joe. "You do the field team, I'll get someone to contact Jan's mother."

Bryan used the radio from one of the county cars to contact the regional FBI office in Chattanooga and told them to get a crew over to the site where the truck was being taken. "I want anything they find, from gum wrappers to cigarette butts. Everything," he ordered. Joe , in the meantime, told the nearest deputy where Kathy was staying and asked him to contact her right away, in person if possible.

The driver's address turned out to be easier to get than they anticipated. Sam's house was not on the main highway up the mountain, but down a narrow, winding, dirt road on the west brow of the mountain. As they drove, Bryan noted ahead a column of black smoke twisting its way into the sky, an ominous sign of things to come. By the time they got there, the house where they supposed Sam Daniel's had been staying had completely burned down. There were a couple of fire trucks from the Signal Mountain Fire Department on the site, but little was left other than a large pile of hissing grey ash. Bryan walked over to a fireman wearing a white slicker, signifying he was the firechief, and began to question him about the fire.

"What do you know about all this?" Bryan asked.

"It was definitely set. The house was all wood, and an accelerant was used in several places. A large propane tank near the house blew. She went up in a flash."

"The person who lived here," said Bryan, "was killed in a wreck on the S-curve at approximately 6 a.m. You think this happened roughly the same time?"

"Yeah," the fire chief answered. "I think that pretty likely."

Bryan returned to the car where Joe was standing, surveying the havoc wreaked by the fire. "Doesn't look like we'll find much here," Joe said, shaking his head.

"No, not much left."

As they walked together toward what little was left of the house, Bryan filled in his partner about the possibility of arson. There was little doubt in his mind as to the reason it was torched.

"Whoever did this did not intend to leave anything behind," Bryan said. "All we can hope for are some clues from the truck, or that Sam was carrying something on him that we can use."

Joe walked back to the car. "Man, this all happened so fast. This poor guy has lived up here for the past twenty years, we find a skull in the lake, and the next thing you know, he's dead, and his house is destroyed."

"On the way back down the mountain, let's stop at the wreck site again and tell the sheriff's people about this fire. Ask him to send our lab people up here after they finish with the wreck," said Bryan.

It was decided that Joe would go to the lab, where the autopsy on the body had apparently begun, and see if it was yielding anything useful. On the way, he would drop off Bryan at Jan's parents' hotel where Bryan could talk with Jan's parents and call Jan. Bryan was anxious to find out where Sam Daniels fit into this story.

Bryan knocked on Kathy's door and she opened after the second knock. She was already dressed and ready for the day. She spoke to him after she opened the door. "Well, well, Inspector Langston." She smiled and said, "Jan described you so well, I would have known you without the introduction. That's the journalist in her. It's good to see you this morning. What's going on?" As he entered the room, she told him that Jan had arrived and had gone downstairs to get some breakfast. She was due back anytime now, but while they waited, Kathy asked how the case was coming along.

He told her about the wreck on Signal Mountain and about the related fire, then asked her if she had any recollection of Sam Daniels that might have given an indication as to why someone would want him dead. He told her that there was reason to believe that someone was trying to destroy some evidence and people related to Larry's murder.

She looked shocked and replied, "Oh, my God, Bryan. We talked to a man named Sam yesterday. He told Beth and me that he worked on the TVA project at Watts Bar with a guy named Dan, who knew Larry. But he didn't tell us much of anything."

Bryan was even more curious about the wreck, and how it all fit together. He was momentarily distracted when Jan reentered the room, and his attention was drawn to her tight-fitting capris.

Kathy and Bryan told her about what had occurred that morning. She agreed with them that it was too convenient for the house to go up the same morning the truck went off the mountain.

"I would bet anything that the brakes were tampered with or something else mechanically done to that truck," Bryan said as he stood up and offered his chair to Jan.

"Well," said Kathy, "when the deputy came in and told us to stay in our rooms until further notice, I knew that something bad had happened."

"So, Inspector," Jan said to Bryan, "what do we do next?"

"I think the important thing right now is for you to stay with your mother and for the two of you to stay out of harm's way," said Bryan as he looked into Jan's eyes and then over at her mother. "I'll put someone outside in the hallway just to be safe."

Bryan pulled a chair from the periphery of the room and sat down next to Jan, so the three of them could communicate easier. Then he looked over at Kathy and began to question her in more detail about Larry, and about how Dan fit into the picture.

Chapter 19
Chattanooga, same day

A soft knock at the door and the door opened slowly. Jan's father, Frank, entered carrying a tray with a plastic thermal carafe and white styrofoam cups. Also on the tray were a sugar container and a cream dispenser. He set the tray down on the table beside them, held his hand out his hand to Bryan and introduced himself.

Jan introduced Bryan to her dad, smiling at Bryan as she did so.

"Seems like I already know you, Bryan," confessed Frank. "Our daughter has told us all about you."

"Good things, I hope," joked Bryan as he stood and stepped forward into the middle of the room to shake his hand.

They filled Frank in as to what had happened and told him that they were discussing Larry's past. Bryan indicated to Frank to join them.

"Let me pour us all some coffee," Frank offered. "I know how the ladies like theirs. How about you, Bryan?"

"Just black, please," answered Bryan.

They sat in the chairs surrounding a small coffee table and began to talk about what had transpired that morning. Bryan told them about the crash on Signal Mountain and about the corresponding fire at Sam's house on top of the mountain. He could see the fear come across

Kathy's face as he recounted the events of the day to her husband, and she held tightly to Frank's hand.

"This Sam Daniels fellow. What can you tell me about him?" Bryan asked Kathy.

"Yesterday was the first time that I ever met him," she said. "He was a co-worker of a friend of ours from the old neighborhood. They worked together on the TVA project at Watts Bar." She shrugged as if that was all she knew.

"Just take your time and tell me whatever you can about him."

"He really didn't say too much about his relationship with Dan, that was the friend I was talking about," she said. "I know they used to ride together to work at Watts Bar, and Dan mentioned him a couple of times."

"Who is this Dan you are talking about?" asked Bryan.

"He and his wife, Phyllis, used to live next to us. We all went to high school together," Kathy said. "Well, Phyllis and Dan went to Central High School, and Larry and I went to City. They played football against each other every year and became and stayed friends after high school. Phyllis and I weren't really close friends in high school. She graduated a year ahead of me and I really never knew her. They had a son, he was about six years old when Phyllis and Dan got a divorce and she moved away. I think his name was Billy."

"So, what did Dan do before working with the TVA?" asked Bryan.

"His dad was a plumber, and Dan worked for him for a while after high school. After Larry went into the Navy, Dan got a job with the TVA."

"Do you remember anything else about him?" asked Bryan.

"After Larry enlisted and Dan started having problems with

Phyllis, Dan became infatuated with me," she confessed. Her eyes dropped to her lap, as if not wanting to look them in the face.

"How close did the relationship become?"

"Much closer for him than for me. I reacted to Dan because I needed someone to talk to, and he was part of our life before," she said.

"I don't want to get too personal right now, but how close did it get?"

Kathy did not want to reveal too much about her hidden past affair with Dan and she told him that there were no intimate feelings in the relationship on her part. She did tell him that Dan was very intrusive and always coming by her house. Toward the end of the time she knew him, he had become so obsessed with their relationship that she sought ways to avoid him and actually hid from him with Beth's help.

"Did you have any contact with him after Larry disappeared?"

"No," she said. "After Larry disappeared, seemingly lost in the war, I made every effort to stay away from him. To be honest, I was really afraid of him by then."

"So you have no knowledge of what became of Dan after 1941?"

"All I know is what I learned yesterday. An old neighbor said he would drive past my house daily for a while after I moved away, and Sam told Beth and me that they were in the war together in North Africa or somewhere. When they got home, he came back to Chattanooga, and Dan went to South Florida somewhere to work with his brother in the salvage business."

"Did he say where in South Florida, or mention the name of the business?"

"No," she answered. "The only thing he said was that a group of them from the war got together every few years for a reunion somewhere."

"I need you to tell me," said Bryan, "what you can remember when you learned of Larry's disappearance."

She told him about the letter she had received from Larry. "He had been given leave to come home for a week or so on December 6th or 7th, depending on the connections he could make. When he didn't show up as scheduled, I just assumed that he had gotten delayed and was still in Pearl Harbor when the Japanese attacked. He was aboard the *Oklahoma*, which was one of the ships hardest hit."

She stopped for a minute to wipe her eyes with a tissue and take a sip of coffee, then continued, "There were a lot of sailors on that ship who could not be identified, so we assumed one of them was Larry."

"There were no records of him leaving port before the attack?"

"I asked that same question to the Navy," Kathy said. "They told me that most of the records of the week leading up to the attack were probably still on board and had not been filed yet."

"Could Larry have come home earlier than that date without you knowing?"

She told him about the lost letter, and confessed that there could have been something in that letter about coming in earlier. There was no telephone call or telegram from him at all. She told him about the circumstances of the lost letter and how she was so upset about Dan being there, that she did not realize that she had lost the letter until she got home.

"So," said Bryan, "you could have dropped the letter, and Dan could have found it, read it, and never told you about it?"

"That's certainly possible," she agreed.

"Can you stay put here for a while until we can get some

answers?" he asked her. "I'm really afraid for you to be out, even with someone following you for protection. Until we find out who it is and how it all fits together, you would be much safer in here, with the guard posted outside."

"That's not what I want to do," she answered, "but I will. It might be a good idea to keep Jan with me, too."

He nodded. "I don't think she would be in danger, but you can't ever tell."

He turned to Jan. "Why don't you stay here with your parents and I'll take your rental car and start running down some of this new information? I'll call you and keep you guys in touch with what is going on."

He turned back to Kathy and said, "I know that you will want to make arrangements to have Larry buried. There is a veterans' cemetery here over on Bailey Avenue where they would handle the arrangements for you. Why don't you give them a call? I'm sure they will be ready to release the remains in a day or two."

"Thanks, Bryan," she answered. She handed over the keys to her rental car. "I'll do that."

He nodded in acknowledgment. "Only, I've got to stay here until Joe calls me and we can meet up somewhere. I told him I would be here," Bryan said as he reached for the door.

"Well, why don't you go ahead and we can tell Joe where you are," said Jan. "I need to stay here with Mom for a while. You can just bring the rental back here when you finish."

"Okay," said Bryan. "I'm going to the records office of the U.S. Army and see if I can find the names of some of the people nearby who served with Dan. Too many things seem to connect back to him."

149

Purple Haze

Chapter 20
Memphis, 1970

William Bowers assured him that he would take care of the problem. Billy, the name he preferred to be called, had been raised by his dad after his mother died while he was still in college. He had become very close to his dad over the past few years and felt a strong obligation to help whenever he needed him. Billy really had no idea what the source of the problem was, and he really didn't want to know. He only knew that there was an individual in Chattanooga that had some information about his dad that would be very harmful and needed to be destroyed.

His dad knew that he had the contacts to take care of the situation and that he would do whatever was needed to cover his back. Billy called a contact he had in Chattanooga, told him exactly what needed to be done, and it was taken care of within the day. He was satisfied that the job had been completed and that there was no evidence to link him or his father to the crime. Afterwards, he called his dad in Florida to tell him what had been done.

"Hey, Dad," he began. "That problem you wanted to clear up in Chattanooga has been taken care of. There's no evidence."

"That's good news, son," answered Dan. "What do I owe you, Billy?"

"Hey, this is family," answered Billy. "You don't owe me a thing. Let me know if you need anything else done. This guy I've got in Chattanooga is very reliable and works quick."

Billy leaned back in his swivel chair and lit up a big Cuban cigar that he had gotten from one of his "friends" in Miami. He was proud that his dad was pleased. Billy had built a successful business in Memphis in a restaurant called "Billy Boy's" and he had partial ownership in a construction company, but he also had a powerful cartel of friends in other businesses that ran outside the law, including prostitution and drugs.

"There might be another loose end that needs to be tied up," his dad said to him.

"What is it, Pop?"

"There's a lady that I used to know who I need to find. I don't want her killed off or anything like that, I just need to know where she is."

"Okay, tell me what you know and I'll get my people working on it."

"I lost contact with her during the war and when I got home, I couldn't find any traces of her, except that she had moved to Nashville while I was overseas. I guess the best starting place would be there."

"What's the name, Pop?" he asked.

"Her name was Kathy Gibson when she moved away from here between early 1942 and when I returned to the states in 1943. She had a daughter and at last account I heard was she was in Nashville and had gotten married to an insurance executive named Frank Goodson."

"Well, that will give me a starting place at least."

"Call me if you find anything," Dan said, "or if you need any more information. Thanks a lot."

After he had hung up the phone, Billy called his contact in Chattanooga, and made arrangements to wire him the money for payment after receiving the details on the completed job. Then he asked him to look into Kathy Gibson.

"Okay, Billy," said the man on the other end, Paul. "I'll get right to work on it. When you get the details on the money, contact me at the Hotel Patten, room 212."

"Let me know if there are any problems."

"I will do that."

Paul Odom had been working as an independent "fixer" for the past ten years and had earned a reputation as someone who could solve a problem quickly and leave no trail. The way he had handled the hit on Sam Daniels was an example of his efficiency. He had followed Sam to his house that evening, and after he had gone to sleep, Paul cut the brake lines on Sam's truck. He then waited for Sam to leave his house that morning, and had set fire to his house about thirty minutes later. If there had been any trace of a phone message or other information, it was all burned up in the fire.

Paul didn't know too much about Chattanooga. He worked out of Atlanta and had taken a flight into town the day before, rented a car under one of his assumed identities, and had taken care of his business. He had been waiting around for the call from Billy before he left town. After the call, he got right to work on his next job. Before Paul had begun working in his present trade, he had taken a job with a lawyer in Atlanta working as a research assistant. In that position, he had learned a lot about how to find information on people. He was particularly good at finding people who did not want to be found. It seemed that the search for Kathy Gibson was going to be one of those jobs.

By noon, Paul had discovered that Kathy Gibson, now Kathy

Goodson, had lived in Chattanooga from 1940 through the early part of 1942. She had married a Lawrence Gibson, and they lived together in Avondale, and Lawrence had joined the Navy in 1941. He soon discovered that his was the body that had recently been discovered in the nearby lake. This search for Kathy Gibson had connected for him the jobs that he was now working. He still had not discovered how Sam Daniels fit into everything, but he was sure that he would. Even though the reasons behind the job were not really important to him, he always had a desire to know as much about the background of the job as possible. He figured there might come a time when it would be important to know.

That evening while Paul was watching the local news broadcast from his hotel room, he discovered that Kathy Goodson was in Chattanooga. He also learned that there was to be a burial service for Lawrence Gibson at the Veterans' Cemetery in two days. He now had a great deal of news to share with Billy when he called him later that night. He decided to take some of the time that he had before Billy's call to walk down to the Read House where he knew Kathy Goodson was staying and see if he could figure out how to get to her if the need arose. It was just a short walk to the Read House and he was immediately surprised to see that there were visible police cars around the hotel and that there were officers inside the hotel in the lobby. As he walked the stairways and looked out on each of the floors, it appeared that she was on the third floor, because that was where a number of officers were stationed. He walked back down the stairs and through the lobby without looking back, and then down the street toward his hotel.

He stopped at a coffee shop on Market Street on his way back to the Patten and got a large cup to go. He took his coffee and sat at an outside table along the street to kill a little time. He was also curious about how many officers were permanently stationed and how many came and left. After sitting for about twenty minutes, he left and walked back to his room. Within a short time, his phone rang.

He told Billy what he had found out about Kathy and how she fit in to the story on the news of the Navy person found in the lake. He told him about the protection that was around the hotel where she was staying. He also told him about the funeral that would be coming up in a couple of days. Billy thanked him and told him to sit tight until he got back to him. He told him that he would hear from him again tomorrow night, and asked him to find out anything else he could about Kathy Goodson.

Purple Haze

Chapter 21
Chattanooga, 1970

On his way out to the parking lot of the Read House, Bryan decided to make a few phone calls from a pay phone in the lobby using his FBI card. His first call was to a friend of his he met in training who had decided not to go into law enforcement, but instead had gone into the Army. Jack Tollitson worked with the National Archives and Records Administration in Washington, D.C., and would be a good starting point for his search. After Tollitson came to the phone, he explained what he needed.

"Hey, Jack," he began. "This is Bryan Langston. How's the Army treating you these days?"

"Kind of hectic right now, trying to keep up with all the Vietnam data we have coming in," Jack answered. "What can I do for you?"

"Where would I find Army records for a person who served in North Africa during World War II?" he asked.

"Our records here only go back to Korea and the 1950s," he answered. "I have a friend who works with the National Personnel Records Center, who has access to all the Military personnel files-- might take a day or two. I'll contact her for you and get her to work on it. Give me what information you have and I'll run it by her."

"Really, Jack," he answered, "I don't have a whole lot except a name, city of origin, and an approximate date."

"Okay, buddy," he answered. "Give those to me and we'll see."

"His name is Dan Bowers." Bryan looked at his notes and continued. "It would have been 1942, maybe the early part of the year, from Chattanooga. I think he shipped out to somewhere in North Africa."

"Okay, got it all," Jack said. "What information do you need?"

"What would really help are some names of people with whom he served, maybe in the same company, especially those that lived in the southeast around Tennessee. I've also got the name Sam Daniels. I know he served with him there."

"That's a big help," Jack said. "One of the problems we have with World War II records is that there was a fire in the records building where some of the information for that time period was stored."

"Well, see what you can find, and get back with me," Bryan said. "I'll give you the number where I am staying and you can call me there or leave a message and I'll call you back."

"Will do, Bryan. Good to hear from you."

"You, too, Jack. Thanks for your help."

After he hung up the phone, the next call he had to make was to the sheriff's department, to see if he could get into contact with anyone in the lab. After going through a couple of extensions, he was finally able to locate Joe, who was still in forensics, going over the body of Sam Daniels. He told him to sit tight and that he would come by there and they could get together to compare notes.

"Why don't you just let me pick you up?" asked Joe. "I'm through here, and we will only have to fool with the one car that way."

"Good idea," agreed Bryan. "I'll take the keys back upstairs to Jan, and I'll wait for you in front of the hotel. You're what, about fifteen minutes away?"

"Give or take a little, depends on the traffic. See you then."

After giving the keys back to Jan, he went back through the lobby and out the glass doors onto Market Street. After a few minutes, Joe parked in front of the hotel and Bryan got into the car.

As the car was pulling away from the curb, they began to compare notes on what information they had gathered thus far. Bryan told Joe about what he found out about Dan Bowers and his relationship with Sam Daniels. He also told him that he had contacted a friend of his in the military to search for information on Dan and his battalion mates. He still wanted to contact the Veterans Administration to get up-to-date material on him.

Joe shared with Bryan what he had found out about the wreck on Signal Mountain earlier that morning. The brake lines had indeed been cut, and that brake failure was the cause of the accident. They found no evidence of drugs on the body, or any evidence that there had been any physical cause, such as a heart attack, that could have contributed to the wreck. He told him that the Hamilton County Sheriff's Department was listing the death as homicide. He said that there was no evidence of any kind found on the body, except a wallet with a slip of paper with a Florida telephone number scratched on it. The number had traced to a salvage company in Jupiter, Florida.

The fact that the salvage company was owned by a person named Timothy Bowers definitely tied the telephone number to the Dan Bowers they'd learned about. They agreed that he was a key person in the investigation and decided to concentrate their efforts on him. They also needed to go to the crime scene in Rhea County to see if anything new had turned up at the recovery dive.

"Let's go by the sheriff's department here before we head up that way," Bryan said, "I need to touch base with Jan and let them all know where we will be if they need us."

"That's a good idea," said Joe. "I can check with the Hamilton County people to see if they have put together anything else we could use."

At the Sheriff's department, Joe was directed to Lieutenant Watson, who was in charge of the case and Bryan was given the use of a detective's desk in the main office, where he could make his telephone call.

Jan answered the telephone.

"Hello," she answered warily.

"Hey, Jan," said Bryan. "Joe and I are headed up to Dayton to check on the recovery effort and see if anything new has been found. I've also got the name of a man who was in the same army group with Bowers and may have worked with him."

"Okay," answered Jan. "When do you think you guys will be back in town?"

"Oh, I'd say four or five hours, maybe six o'clock," he answered. "Why don't I give you a call then, and we can go out to eat?"

"I'll be in my motel room then, so call me there," she said. "There's not much going on here, and Mom and Dad are getting a little antsy."

"Let me talk to your mom a minute."

Jan handed the phone to her mom and Kathy said hello.

"Mrs. Goodson, I see no reason why you and your husband can't go out and do what you want to do. Just be sure and tell one of the deputies so they can get someone to stay close by."

"That's great," replied Kathy. "We were just talking about going out to get something to eat and maybe go to see the movie *Patton*. I was reading that it's on at the Tivoli Theater close to here. We could even walk over there from the hotel."

"Yeah, that'll be great," said Bryan. "Just be sure the deputies know where you are going."

"Okay, Agent Langston. Thanks for all your help."

She handed the phone to Jan, who secured plans with Bryan for the evening.

After he hung the phone up, he walked back to Detective Watson's desk where Joe was involved in a conversation about the case. He had a group of crime scene photos in front of him of the wreck and the burnt out house on Signal Mountain. It was obvious that the two incidents were related but there had been no evidence found in either incident. They had one witness in the arson case that saw a light-colored Chevy Nova driving away from the house about the time of the fire. It was early in the morning and it was foggy, so she was unable to tell the officers much, except that it looked like a Nova because her son drove the same car in a darker shade. She did not pay attention to the plate or the driver, and she only remembered it because it was unusual for any vehicle except Sam's to be coming from that direction. According to the report, she was walking back to her house after milking, and saw it as it passed in front of her house.

"Call the deputies over at the Read House and give them a description of the car and tell them to be aware of it," said Bryan.

"We'll do that," said the detective. "Let us know if we can help you anymore."

"Thanks," said Joe, "we'll do that."

Joe picked up the phone on the desk and dialed the Rhea County Sheriff's Department number from a card Sheriff Robinson had given him on the barge the day before. After he got Robinson on the phone, he was told that they had closed down the dive site and that they were getting all the materials together to ship out to the forensic lab in Nashville. He told him that the case had been placed on high priority and that they were going to do all the tests overnight and should have some answers by the next day.

"We're heading that way right now," said Joe. "We need to see what you got and see if there's anything related to what's going on here." Joe gave him the details of what had happened the past twenty-four hours and told him that there appeared to be a link but they didn't know what it was. He was told that the recovery materials had been documented and photographed and that they were welcome to look over all that material.

"The real stuff is already packed up and loaded and ready to go," said Robinson.

"That's okay," said Joe. "Is the diver still there?"

"Yeah," he answered. "I'll tell him to wait until you guys get here, if you want."

"Thanks. See you within the hour."

Chapter 22
Jupiter City, Florida, 1970

Nothing made Dan Bowers more nervous than having a problem and having no way to control it. All you could do was to give the job to someone you trusted and hope that it would be taken care of. Even though Sam had been his closest friend and someone he had served beside in the war, the news about him being out of the picture was good for Dan. He did not feel Sam's death would provide any direct links to him other than knowing him. There was no way to trace the accident or the fire to him. But he was becoming more and more anxious about the investigation concerning Larry's body. It was amazing that the body had stayed hidden for thirty years and now it was discovered.

Looking back to the night of the crime, it seemed perfect. No one except him even knew Larry was coming home early and no one except he and Sam knew what had happened that night. Larry's bus was supposed to come into the Southern Bus Company station at 11 p.m. and Sam met him at the station. Dan had told Sam nothing about what he was planning, and had never discussed it with him at all afterwards. After Sam had dropped Larry off at the motel, Dan had taken Larry from the motel toward the hospital, supposedly to get into Kathy's room through an orderly that Dan knew.

Purple Haze

It had been early in the morning when Dan pulled the truck off Market Street under the bridge.

Dan had told Larry that they still had a little time to kill and suggested that they go down by the river under the bridge and drink a beer like the old days. Larry, who was still unwinding from the long trip, felt that a beer was just what he needed. Larry exited the truck and walked straight toward the river's edge unsuspectingly, with his back to Dan.

Dan had a .22 revolver with a sweater wrapped around it hidden in his hand. The sweater not only hid the gun but muffled the sound, when he discharged it into the back of Larry's head.

Death was instant. Larry slumped to the ground without a sound.

Dan used a canvas tarp from the back of his truck to rolled the body in, then threw the revolver into the river and drove away.

Being careful not to speed or call any attention to himself, he drove up Highway 27 to Dayton and then to the construction site. He passed a sheriff's car in Red Bank and there was another one on the county line before he got into Rhea County near Dayton. As he passed each of the cars, his eyes stayed focused both on the road and on the rear view mirror to see if either of them was turning around. At the early hour he arrived in Dayton, there was no traffic and not a single vehicle was on the road to the construction site. He stopped his truck outside the construction site fence and looked under a large stone for a hidden key that the foreman had placed there for after-hours emergencies. He drove through the gate, locked it behind him and took the key. He drove past the construction trailer and into the excavated lake bed, deeper and deeper into the hole that was to soon be Watts Bar Lake. The day before he had set a large metal and wood form that had been used to make the concrete blocks for the dam itself. These forms had been partially buried and left at the bottom of the lake bed to be covered with water. This particular one was about half full of rock and stood about eight feet tall. He backed his truck up to the form and used a ladder he had put in his truck that day to lean against the form. He carried Larry's body covered by the tarp up the ladder and dumped it on top of the rock in the form. He spent the next couple of hours loading large stones into the back of his truck, then he backed the truck up to the form again, and began tossing the stones on the body. When he was satisfied that the body was completely covered, he pulled his truck a few hundred feet away and smoothed out the ground so there would be no tracks visible.

He drove out of the lake bed, went through the construction gate, relocked the gate behind him and drove toward Dayton. He had seen no one and had passed no vehicles coming out of the area or driving into it. He knew that they were going to begin filling the lake on Monday and if he could get the body hidden and covered it would be buried under fifty or sixty feet of water by the end of the week.

The fitting climax to this perfect crime occurred when the Japanese attacked Pearl Harbor and all those sailors had lost their lives, including Larry Gibson, who never showed up for his scheduled leave.

The only flaw in his happy ending had been that he did not end up with the one thing he wanted the most. After the murder, he had tried to stay clear of Kathy as long as possible, allowing her to believe that Larry had been delayed in port and was lost at Pearl Harbor, with the other 2,000 or more who perished there. But he had allowed her to elude him for too long, and she was able to avoid seeing him out of what he thought was the guilt of carrying his child, with her husband dying in the war. That had been too much of a burden for Kathy to carry, and she had successfully dropped out of sight.

He did not find her until her name appeared among a list of war widows who had attended the ceremony dedicating the new cemetery at what was called Punchbowl National Cemetery in Hawaii. He was disappointed to see that she had remarried and that their child was now the child of an insurance executive in Nashville. But he knew that the child would always be *their* child. He just had no idea how long it would take and what would be involved in his reunion with his rightful family.

After Dan had returned home from the war, he decided to join his brother in Jupiter, Florida who operated a salvage business. He had always been fascinated with diving, and his knowledge of welding and metal working had made it the perfect job.

They had turned the business into a successful enterprise. But in his personal life, Dan had not remarried, and had no lasting relationships with anyone. He always tried to stay up to date on what was happening with Kathy and their daughter. In spite of what he had told Billy, he had made several trips to Nashville and had watched his daughter grow up and was present when she graduated from both high school and college. He was curious as to what his son could dig up on her life in Nashville that he did not know about. It was enough for him to stay unseen, and to remain in the background. Now, it seemed that that idea was about to change.

Dan was certain that his relationship with Kathy was about to be discovered, and that he had to take whatever steps necessary to insure that their secret remained their secret. He was also certain that a trip back to Chattanooga was going to be necessary; what had to be done now could not be done by someone else. Even as efficient as Billy's friend had been, this was a job he was going to have to see through to the end himself. He took what information Billy had given to him about where Kathy was staying and the amount of security around, and decided that the best place to make a move was the memorial service, but in order to do what he had planned, it was going to take some help.

He picked up the phone on his desk and called Billy.

"Hey Billy Boy," he said as he answered. "I've decided to make a trip up your way to take care of some business."

"Sure, Pop," he answered. "What do you need on this end?"

"I don't want to get you any more involved in this, so I've got a plan here to solve my problem and keep you out of it as much as possible."

"Okay, what do you need?"

"I need you to leave me a car parked at the airport in Chattanooga, make sure it's not a rental car or one that can be traced back to you. You call me with a description of the car when you get one, and place a hidden key in one of those magnetic boxes under the driver's side front wheel well."

"I can do that for you," said Billy. "What else?"

"Get in touch with your guy that took care of that other situation for me, and set up a place to meet me after I get in town."

"After you call me back with the flight schedules, I'll get Paul set up somewhere where you can meet and talk. What are your plans, Pop?"

"The less you know about it the better," answered Dan. "The FBI is going to be watching you if they're on to me. So let's just leave it unknown for now. If you'll take care of those things for me, I'll handle the rest and get back out of town before anyone knows I'm there."

After he hung up the phone, he called Delta and booked a flight from Tampa to Chattanooga in the early morning hours, the day after tomorrow. That would give him a day to get all of his plans worked out without any major complications. He booked the flight under the name Tom Bradford with a credit card he used for illegal purposes or when the need arose. The card had been provided to him by his brother when he went to work for him because sometimes in their line of work, he needed another identity. He told his brother that he was going to have to go out of town for a few days to take care of some business, and that he should return for the weekend. He told him that if anyone called looking for him, to tell them that he was in Houston, Texas and should return by Saturday. The fact that Dan had lived alone after the war was an asset for him in times like these. If he could cover his tracks with his brother, he would be home free. He then called Delta Airlines for the second time and booked a flight for midday tomorrow to Houston, and used his own name and credit card. He had no intention of showing up for that flight, but a record of the transaction would be there in case anyone checked.

Chapter 23
Dayton, July 9, 1970

It took Joe and Bryan a little less than an hour to arrive at the sheriff's office in downtown Dayton. Jerry Standridge, the diver who had worked the scene from the beginning, was waiting on them to arrive and they began talking immediately about what had been left on the bottom of the lake. After talking with the forensic people on site, and with the TVA engineers, Jerry had drawn several conclusions based on the evidence he saw. The body had apparently been thrown into the form after a foot or more of rock had been placed in the bottom, and three to four feet of rock had been thrown in on top of the body. Through the years, due to flooding or other natural causes, the body had worked its way loose enough for a part of it—the skull—to float free. Standridge was convinced by the way it was done that it would have had to have been someone who had access to the site and that it was most likely a man, since women only had administrative jobs with the TVA lakes project. "It could even have been two men," Standridge continued. "Judging from the original height of the form, getting a body that high off the ground would have required a lot of strength from one man."

"And enough strength to cover the form with enough rocks that it wouldn't be seen before the lake was filled. So," Joe said, turning to

169

Bryan, "it would have had to occur on the few days before the lake was filled up, possibly even the night before."

"That sounds right, Joe," agreed Bryan. "We'll need to get with the TVA and establish a timeline, and get them to give us a list of who was still on the site at that time."

They spent some time going over the documents concerning the search, the map of the dive—with the areas marked where certain things were found—and the Polaroid photos of the artifacts themselves. There was nothing new. The talk with the diver had been the most useful information and the search tomorrow was going to concentrate on locating and interviewing as many of the workers as they could locate. They knew that one of them, Sam Daniels, had already been taken out, so they had to work quickly.

Before leaving Dayton, Bryan called Jan's room to finalize plans for the evening and she answered quickly on the first ring.

"I was hoping that was you," she said as soon as she picked up.

"I was just checking in to see what you wanted to do tonight."

"What did you have in mind?"

"It's six right now," answered Bryan, "Why don't you come by my room and pick me up at, say, eight? Is that too late?"

"No, no," she replied. "Eight would be just fine. See you then."

"See you."

He hung up and walked back to where Joe was talking to the diver. He was asking him a few more questions about the positioning of the form, and its relationship to the shore. It was conclusive after the discussion that the crime was committed on the day before the lake was filled, possibly after hours or sometime during the weekend before the onset of flooding the lake bed. Their best guess was the Sunday night or early Monday morning before the water was released upstream.

They left the Dayton sheriff's office with the idea to find addresses and locations of some of Sam's and Dan's fellow workers. The main offices of the TVA were located in Chattanooga, so it should not be too difficult to find the old construction records from 1941. The difficult part would be tracing the whereabouts of those people after thirty years.

Jan arrived right on time that evening. She and Bryan went to an upscale Greek restaurant on the north side of town called The Acropolis. The food was delicious and the atmosphere was very relaxing. After they left the restaurant, they went to a nearby group of cinemas and bought tickets for *Love Story*. The movie was scheduled to start in thirty minutes, so they sat on a bench in the mall and talked about their day.

"Mom was really worried about what was happening," Jan said. "She said that she felt bad that all this was being brought back to life after thirty years. She was very upset that the man was murdered that they had talked with. She said it was her fault."

"It wasn't, and no one is blaming her," said Bryan. "We would have found him and talked to him ourselves soon. His name would have been part of the investigation we're beginning now. It was obvious from the evidence at the dive site that whoever murdered your dad was someone who worked on the construction crew that excavated the lake and built the dam. We're beginning the search tomorrow morning and working through everyone we can find."

"I can't believe this is happening," exclaimed Jan. "For all these years, my father has been buried in that lake! It's just unbelievable."

"I think it is very important that you and your mom take it easy until we can get to the bottom of all this. One person has already died, and it's obvious that whoever murdered your father is not going to stop until everyone who knows anything is destroyed also. I'm afraid that may include your mother, and therefore, you also." He stood and took hold of her hand. "Come on, let's head into the theater, it's time for the movie."

They sat close together in the movie and held hands from start to finish. By the time the movie ended, everyone was crying, and they could see people with red eyes and tissues walking out into the parking lot. They walked to Jan's car. Bryan felt the hair on his neck and arms tingle as if they were being followed or in danger somehow.

"Don't turn around," he instructed, "but I think we're being followed. After you get into the car, drive around the mall parking lot twice and see if there are any cars following."

She did as instructed and kept her eyes on the rear view mirror. There was a black Plymouth that followed them halfway around the first time, but after the second lap, there was no one behind them.

"Go out to the red light and turn left back toward downtown."

She did that, and drove at the speed limit back into town. They went through the tunnel at Missionary Ridge, and back out toward town. Bryan was finally convinced that they were not being followed.

"It's really getting late, Bryan," said Jan. "Why don't we go back to the hotel and see if Mom and Dad are back yet?"

"That's a good idea, let's do that."

They parked in front of the hotel and walked past a couple of deputies who told them that everything had been quiet. They said that the Goodson's had come back about thirty minutes ago and had gone straight to their room. Jan and Bryan decided that it was too late to go up and bother them.

"Look, Jan," began Bryan. "Joe and I are going to start doing some researching tomorrow on some of these TVA workers and their whereabouts. I know you said that would you like to help us with some of the digging. Does that still apply?"

"Sure," answered Jan. "You know how reporters are."

"Well, I know that most are good at research and digging, and that's what this is."

"What time are you guys going to get going?"

"The TVA offices don't open until nine or so, so we'll come by and pick you up at eight and we'll go get some breakfast."

"It would probably be better if we had both cars," Jan replied. "Why don't I meet you at the restaurant at your motel at 7:30?"

"That sounds like a deal. Let's get me back to my room so I can hit the hay and be ready to go."

They walked back out to Jan's car, and drove back through town and straight to Bryan's motel. After Jan dropped off Bryan, she continued to drive to her motel and parked her car in front of her room, got out and locked her car door and unlocked the room as the driver of a light blue Nova wrote down all the information on a note pad he had on the front seat.

After she entered the room and got ready for bed, her phone rang.

"Hello," she said in the receiver.

"Hey, Jan," said Bryan. "I was just checking to see if you got in all right."

"Everything's fine," answered Jan, unaware of the person sitting in her parking lot at the same time she was saying it.

"See you in the morning, then," he said. "Sleep well."

"You, too, Bryan. Good night."

Purple Haze

Chapter 24
Jupiter, Florida, July 9, 1970

Dan filled his lungs with cool morning sea air as he jogged along the beach. One of the things that had kept him in good physical condition was his regimen of running, eating healthy, and staying away from alcohol. As Dan ran along the deserted beach, just as the sun was rising in the east beyond the barrier island, he was thinking about what he had to do. He had lived in relative peace for the past thirty years, and now suddenly his peaceful world was being shattered by something that he had done dispassionately years ago. Now that impetuous act was going to have to be covered up by other acts that he really had no desire to commit. He knew, however, that something had to be done, and it had to be done soon. He could feel the noose tightening around his neck.

He quickened his pace as the tension rose and by the end of his run he was panting heavily and sweating profusely. His stamina was not what it used to be, but for a man in his early fifties, he was in pretty good shape. There were things that he could no longer do, and he knew that in planning the events of the next two days, he was going to have to be careful and precise in his movements. There was help, Billy had taken care of that for him, but the bulk of his plan had to be executed by no one but him.

Purple Haze

Dan had already told his brother that he was taking a few days off, so he wasn't in as much of a hurry to get back to his house as he usually was. He had to make some plans and map out his strategy, and he had to be sure that there would be no hitches. The plans that he had for Kathy and himself had long ago vanished, and although there was still a dream there, he knew that it would never come true as he had planned. What he had dreamed about with Kathy and their child had become someone else's life. Now the reality of his actions was closing in on him—there was nothing left of that dream. All that was left in his heart now was revenge for Kathy's betrayal, and doing whatever it took to keep the truth hidden.

There was really no way of knowing whether the real truth had already come out, or if she had kept their child's paternity hidden. His only hope was that Kathy would still be as adamant about their relationship as she had been then. Knowing Kathy, he was sure that their child had no idea that her real father lived in Jupiter, Florida, far away from it all. Well, that is one thing that he wanted to come out of this more than anything else. He wanted to tell his daughter who she was, and if nothing else came of it all, he had planned in the next two days to tell her with her mother present. He had not seen his daughter for more than three years, since her graduation from college. It was not the ending that he had hoped for, but it was the only clear way for him now.

He had decided to wait and make his move after the memorial service for Larry tomorrow afternoon. Within an hour or so of the service, the police would start rolling back the protection and would let their guard down. That would be the time to make his move. After he got to Chattanooga, he would make his plans and set up a timetable.

He got back to his beach house and poured himself a glass of orange juice as he did every morning after his run. He also had some sliced mango and some cereal as he sat on his deck and looked out over the beach. Just as he was finishing up, his phone rang, and Billy was on the other end.

"Hey, Pop," began Billy. "How're you doing this morning?"

"Doing great, son. And you?"

"Can't complain. Whatcha got going on, Pop?"

"The less you know, the better, right now. Did you get things set up with our friend?"

"Yeah," answered Billy. "I told him to start casing out the hotel where Goodson and her husband are staying and to get a tail on the daughter and get a line on her. I told him to keep his distance and not get made. He's good, Pop. He'll have all the information you need."

"Okay, here's what I want you to tell him," began Dan. "I'll be flying in on a Delta flight from Tampa to Chattanooga that is due to land there at 1:30 a.m. You have the car waiting for me in the long-term parking area as close as possible to the terminal. You got a line on a car?"

"Yeah," answered Billy. "It'll be a white 1970 Cutlass, and it'll have a red card behind the windshield wiper on the driver's side. There will be a key in a magnetic box under the driver's side wheel well."

"Okay, good," replied his dad. "That all sounds great. Tell your buddy to meet me at the Ramada Inn near the airport and to come to Room 132 at 3 a.m."

"Alright, Pop," he said. "I got it. He'll be there. I'll tell him to say 'pizza' after he knocks, so you'll know it's him. You need anything else?"

"Yeah, as a matter of fact, there is one other thing I need," he answered. "Do you have access to any empty warehouses or other old buildings that I could use for a day or two?"

"Yeah, we own a couple of old buildings in Chattanooga that we bought for speculation after they went out of business," answered Billy. "One of them is on the river on the south side of town and there's not much around."

"Is it accessible?"

"Yeah, there's an old road going into the site and a fence around it but the gate is down so you can just drive right up to it."

"Does it have electricity?"

"As a matter of fact, it does, Pop."

"That sounds like a perfect set-up, Billy. Give your man the details on how to find it so we can drive there in the morning."

After he hung up the phone, he went into the house and began packing what he needed for his trip. Dan had always been a collector of sorts with guns and weapons, and had a wide variety of things he could use. He chose a few of his favorite weapons and packed them under his clothes in one of his check-in suitcases, since security would only check his carry-on. The rest of the stuff he needed, he could get in Chattanooga in the morning. He decided to spend the remainder of the day resting and relaxing at home.

He arrived at the airport in Tampa in plenty of time to make his flight. Seeking to blend in as much as possible, he wore an outfit that gave him the appearance of a man of means, going on a leisure trip, perhaps on a short golfing getaway. He was seated in an aisle seat and read a book most of the way to Chattanooga. After they landed, he went to baggage claim and picked up his two bags, and walked directly out to long-term parking and saw the white Cutlass with the red card on the windshield in the front row. He set down his bags and knelt to feel under the wheel well for the hidden key. After he got it, he unlocked the trunk, put the bags in the trunk and got into the car behind the wheel. He drove directly to the nearby Ramada where he had made a reservation under his assumed name. After the usual check in ritual, he returned to his car and parked it front of his room. After unloading his trunk, he checked his watch. He still had a little time, so he drove up the highway, got some take-out food and brought it back to the motel room to eat while he waited for his contact to arrive.

After he had eaten, a knock came to his door. He looked at his watch—2:55.

"Pizza," said the man at the door.

"Just a moment," Dan answered. He looked out the curtains into the parking lot to see if there was anyone else, and opened the door.

Into the room walked a man dressed in a black T-shirt, Levis, and white tennis shoes, with his hair in a crew cut. He appeared to be thirty to thirty-five years of age and stood about five foot eight with a muscular build. He held out his hand and introduced himself.

"Paul," he said.

"Dan. Have a seat." Dan pointed to a chair by the desk.

Paul's movements and gestures gave Dan the idea that he was a person who was sure of himself and knew what he was doing. He made very little eye contact and looked around the room cautiously before he sat down.

"I understand that you have some information to share," began Dan.

"Billy told me to get as much information as I could on Kathy and Jan Goodson."

"That's right," answered Dan. "Whatcha got?"

"Mrs. Goodson is staying at the Read House Hotel downtown and has the protection of county deputies. There is always at least one car that follows them wherever they go. The daughter, on the other hand, is staying in a motel nearby and does not have protection around her. She is, however, spending time with one of the FBI investigators on the case."

"Let's take a ride," said Dan as he rose to walk to the door and handed the keys to Paul. "I want to check out the warehouse."

They got into the Cutlass and Paul drove toward the address that Billy had given him of the abandoned building. Following the directions, they arrived at an old multi-storied brick building that sat close to the river. They drove across old railroad tracks and to the back of the building and got out. Paul took out a small flashlight and they made their way to the back door, which had been chained shut. Dan reached into the bag he was carrying and took out a pair of bolt cutters, cut the chain and the door opened. They walked across the concrete slab floor of the large interior of the old factory and saw an office in the center of the room. They entered the office and turned on a light overhead so they could see what was there. Dan began to unload some of the items from the zippered bag that he had brought with him, along with the bolt cutters. Paul walked around the old office and found a couple of chairs and brought them inside along with a small table.

They walked along the hallway out of the old office that led into the main warehouse and saw a couple of small rooms that they could use also.

"This place looks perfect," said Dan. "Let's go."

Dan led the way back to the Cutlass and they got in and drove back toward downtown. They drove past the Read House to see how many deputies there were on the street, and there appeared to be two cars there. They then drove over to the motel where Jan was staying and saw that it was relatively wide-open.

When they got back to the Ramada, they began to discuss their options and Dan began to outline exactly what he wanted to do.

"I believe our best option," said Dan, "is to grab the daughter at the motel and force the mother to come to us. If we can snatch her, and then contact Kathy after the memorial service, I think there will be less protection around her and less chance of her being followed."

"We have to pick a time when the daughter is alone and her FBI companion is distracted."

"What information do you have on the memorial service?" asked Dan.

"I called the newspaper and got the details on the service. It's supposed to take place at the cemetery on Bailey Avenue at one. The whole service should take less than an hour and they should be back into their rooms by three or so."

"So we've got a little time to get everything in order," said Dan, as he handed a wad of bills to Paul. "Why don't you see if you can rustle up a couple of old mattresses for the ladies to sleep on while we have them there, maybe an ice chest with some water or drinks. Whatever else you think we might need to take out there before this afternoon."

Purple Haze

Chapter 25
Chattanooga July 10, 1970

Jan drove into the parking lot of Bryan's motel at seven the next morning, and parked two spaces down from his room. He came to the door after the second knock, and greeted her with a big smile and a hug. He turned and knocked at the door adjoining his and Joe came out and greeted them. They walked together past the office and into the side door of the adjoining restaurant. Over breakfast, they made plans for the day and outlined their strategy.

"I thought we could all go down to the TVA office and start our search for the construction crew together," suggested Joe. "I think it will be better if Bryan and I do the interviewing and you can help us run down the addresses of the people we find on the search at the TVA."

"Yeah, once we get the names," said Jan, "I could go down to the county tax offices and search through the known addresses to see where they are now."

"I know that'll take some digging," added Bryan. "What time is the memorial service today?"

"It's at one and I told Mom that I would be at her room at noon with some lunch," answered Jan. "I wanted to go with her to the service."

"We'll probably be up the road at that time," said Joe. "Why don't we plan on meeting back here at three and compare notes?"

"That's a good idea," agreed Jan. "I should be able to make that. Give me a call at my motel room and leave a message if you get tied up. I'll check in there before I come over here."

They ate their breakfast and then left the restaurant in separate cars with Jan following them to the TVA office downtown. After identifying themselves, they asked to see construction records for the Watts Bar Dam Project in 1940 to 1941. A secretary directed them into a large room where they could work at a table, and she began to bring the boxes containing the employment records of that time period to them. By the time she had finished, they had three large white boxes that were marked with the same identifying number with time frames of six months each. They started with the box that was marked "July, 1941-December, 1941." That was the time period they believed that the body was placed in the form, just before the lake was filled.

As they read through the progress of the work from July to December, they could see that this was the phase in which preparations were made to actually fill the lake. They turned over to December, 1941, and saw that the work crew was greatly reduced and that those that remained were there when the lake was filled. They found the name Dan Bowers listed at a Chattanooga address, with the name of his wife, Phyllis, and his son, Billy on the enclosed application as next of kin in case of an emergency. They also found the name Sam Daniels with a Signal Mountain address and listed as single. In addition, they found the name Maury Winters, who was listed with a Rhea County address. They wrote down his wife's name, Joan, and the names of his two children, Ted and Mary, ages 3 and 5. They also found the name Roger Bolton on the finishing crew whose address was listed as

184

Athens, Tennessee. He was married to Alice Bolton and they had no children. In addition to these two new names they found six more that worked with Dan and Sam throughout the construction. They wrote down all those names and last known addresses to research.

After they finished, Joe and Bryan took the information on the two workers out of town in Rhea County and in Athens and decided to head north to begin their search. Jan took the names and addresses of five workers who lived in Hamilton County when the project ended to research there. She spent the next three hours chasing down last known addresses and next of kin to the names she was given. Two of the men had died within the past few years, one of them had moved to Ohio, and the last two were still in the area. She located the ex-wife of one of the men, who told her that her ex-husband was working with the City of Chattanooga. She was able to locate the crew he was working with, but he had no knowledge of what became of Sam Daniels or Dan Bowers. He did give her the name of a friend who had served with them in the army overseas during the war. She wrote down all the information to check out later. The other person with a local address turned out to be someone who lived nearby but was out of town for the week.

Joe and Bryan checked on the two names they had from Rhea County and Athens, and were given a plethora of helpful information. Roger Bolton and his wife Alice sat on their front porch and talked to them about Roger's years with the TVA. He was now working for a large paper producing company in Calhoun just up the road. Luckily, they had caught him on a day when his shift was off the rotation. He remembered Sam Daniels as a good friend and hard worker and someone he could rely on for anything. He and Sam often worked together and had remained good friends after they left the TVA. Roger had not heard about the car accident that had killed Sam and was sorry to hear that he was gone. He said he wanted to check on funeral arrangements and go down and visit the family.

However, his recollection of Dan was not so glowing. According to Roger, Dan was a moody, ill-tempered, hothead, who often had fights with people on the crew. Very few people liked to work with him and he was often alone when he ate his lunch or was on break. He remembered that Sam was about the only person on the crew who had anything good to say about him. He remembered working with Dan a couple of times on assignments, and found him difficult and unreasonable. Joe asked Roger how to get to Dayton from where they were and he told them that they would have to go through Decatur and cross the ferry at the Tennessee River.

"If you catch the ferry right, it only takes about thirty minutes, but if you have to wait on the ferry, it can take an hour or longer," Roger told them.

They thanked both of them for their hospitality and got into their car and drove back through town and out Highway 30 to Decatur and then to the ferry crossing at the river. When they got to the ferry, it was halfway across, headed in the opposite direction, so they knew they would have a little wait.

Bryan walked over to the historical marker by the river to pass the time. "Hey, Joe, did you know the Washington Ferry was named for the town of Old Washington? It's across the river. It's the first town in America named for George Washington."

"That's interesting, Bryan," Joe replied absently, using the time to review their notes. Spending so much time with a history buff like Jan had sparked Bryan's curiosity. Joe's partner turned back to the marker. Bryan relayed the information he read as they waited. The ferry had also been used to take the Cherokees across the river on their way to the council meeting at Rattlesnake Springs, where the fate of the tribe had been decided, resulting in their removal to Oklahoma, the trail they followed becoming known as the Trail of Tears.

When the ferry came back, they drove their car aboard and walked along the railing of the ferry while it crossed. When it reached the other side, they got back in the car and headed into Dayton. They had the address of Maury Winters listed as Rhea County Highway North. They drove down the highway out of town north up Highway 27, and stopped at a grocery store to get help. When they went in the store, the lady who operated the cash register knew Maury Winters and told them that he lived on Smyrna Road, which was about four more miles on the right. She described his house and they thanked her, bought a couple of Cokes and headed up the highway.

They followed the directions past a cemetery and pulled into the gravel driveway of Maury Winters' house. They knocked and Mrs. Winters invited them in and asked them to have a seat in the parlor. Maury came into the house with his straw, wide-brimmed hat on and the two men stood and shook his hand as introductions were made.

"Sure, I remember Dan Bowers," he began. "As sorry a son of a bitch as ever lived. I wouldn't trust him farther than I could spit."

"Anything specific that you can recall?" asked Joe.

"Hell, everything," he answered. "There was just something about him that I just didn't feel good about. I always had the feeling that he was up to something. Y'all know what I mean. You know he's doing something, but you just can't figure out what."

"You worked with him that last week before they finished the project?" asked Bryan.

"Yep, sure did," answered Maury.

"Anything else you can remember about that last couple of weeks?" asked Joe.

"It was a month or so before Christmas and we were riding together in a truck and were supposed to check the fill-up progress of the lake. It was pretty damned weird," he said as he began to scratch his head. "We had the whole damned lake to check and he kept wanting to stay in one little area."

"Why do you think he wanted you to do that? Did he ever say what he was looking for?" asked Bryan.

"No, sir," answered Maury. "I remember that there was a half dozen of those big forms out there in the lake bed and he kept looking at them every time we drove past."

"Where, specifically? Can you recall anything about the spot?"

"I remember it was awfully close to where that town, Rhea Springs, used to be, over in a deep part of the lake bed," answered Maury.

"But you don't recall if he said anything at all about the forms or why he was interested in that area?" asked Joe.

"Nope," answered Maury. "Didn't say a thing about why we kept driving out there. In fact, I asked him once why we had to go back over there and he smarted off about he didn't have to have no damned reason and just told me to do it. So I did."

Mrs. Winters came into the room carrying a tray loaded with glasses and a pitcher of homemade iced lemonade and asked her guests if they would like a little refreshment. Both agents took a glass of the beverage and thanked her for her trouble. She told them to help themselves to some more when they finished and left the tray on the table in front of them. They thanked her again and continued to talk with Maury.

"So, Maury," continued Bryan. "During those last few weeks of work as the lake was being filled, did you notice anything else about Dan Bowers, or did you hear him talking about the forms or the water level at the forms?"

"No sir," he answered, "not really. As I said before, he was real anxious for the lake to be filled."

"Did you have any contact with Dan Bowers or Sam Daniels after the work ended at Watts Bar?" asked Joe.

"I know they got on with the crew working at the Hales Bar project," he answered. "I remember somebody told me that they had joined the army together." Maury didn't know much else beyond that and the interview ended soon after that.

As Bryan and Joe were finishing up, Jan was completing her research around eleven and decided to go back to her motel and freshen up before driving downtown to the Read House to go with her mother and father to the service. She changed into her powder blue three-piece suit with the matching flats. After parking the car in front of the Read House, she made her way to her mother's room. After two knocks, her mother came to the door and greeted her with a hug, and she waved across the room to her father.

"I want you to know," said Jan, speaking to her father, "that you will always be my Dad. I know that this person is my biological father, but you will always be the father I have known for as long as I can remember. It's important to me that you know that."

"I love you, too, Jan," replied Frank. "You have always been my daughter as far as I was ever concerned. I'm so glad that you feel that way, too."

They hugged each other and then the two of them reached out their hands for Kathy's hand and they all hugged.

189

"We're going to get through this day," said Kathy. "I love you both, and I want us to be strong through all this."

The service was brief and very few attended. There was a color guard that gave a military salute and the three of them held hands while the casket with Larry's remains was finally put to rest.

"This is where Larry would want to be buried," said Kathy, weeping. "Not in some crater in Hawaii, or in the bottom of a lake. He's happy here."

They walked slowly away from the cemetery but continued to hold hands until they got to the car. They again hugged each other comfortingly, then got into the car and drove back to the hotel. Jan did not go back up to the room with her parents. She told them that she had to meet Bryan and Joe and headed back to her hotel. When she arrived, she checked with the front desk and found that she had gotten a call from Bryan telling her that they were running late. The message said for her to just wait around her room and they would be there around five.

Chapter 26
Chattanooga, July 10, 1970

Paul followed the car to the cemetery, but remained out of sight. He knew where they were going. He sat in the car in a parking lot across the street and watched the family as they exited the gate of the cemetery and walked back to their car. He paid particular attention to the police cars, and noticed that there was still one car that followed them. He watched closely as the daughter got into her car and drove back to the motel. He passed her en route to the motel, and watched as she went into the office and then came out. He saw that a space had come available in front of her room, which she must have noticed as well, because she moved her car closer before she went into the room and pulled the room drapes closed. Paul waited a little while before he made his move.

He was dressed in a city policeman's uniform when he knocked on her door, and he stood there as she looked out the peephole to identify him before she opened the door. After she unlatched the door and opened it, he pushed the door open and she fell backwards on the bed, as he forced his hand over her mouth to keep her from screaming.

"You stay real quiet," he ordered, "and you won't get hurt."

He had already drenched a handkerchief with ether and he kept it over her mouth as she relaxed and then finally succumbed to the fumes. After she passed out, he looked in her purse for her car keys, and walked out of the room to her car, turned it around, and backed it up to the door of the room. He made sure no one was out walking or that there were no curious neighbors, and after fifteen or twenty minutes he carried her out and placed her into the trunk of her car. He had already decided that it would be better to use her car and to return for his car later. Using her car would make it more difficult to determine that she was missing and would give them more time to put their plan into motion. He drove quietly out of the parking lot and straight to the warehouse where Dan was waiting. Dan had told Paul to keep her out of sight and that Dan would not make himself visible until the plan was well underway.

Paul had placed a mattress on the floor in the old office, and that is where he carried her from the trunk of the car. After he laid her on the mattress, he turned on the overhead light and sat quietly reading a newspaper until she began to stir. She raised her head and looked at the overhead light, then abruptly sat up and saw the man she had opened the door for sitting in the chair nearby.

"What's going on here?" she asked. "Who the hell are you?"

"I think it would be best," he answered, "if you just sit quietly and don't give me a reason to do something I don't want to do."

"Where are we?" she demanded.

"We are in a nice, safe place where no one will ever look, and there is no one for miles around. Screaming and yelling will do you no good."

"What's this all about?" she asked.

"I just do what I'm told," he answered, "and I was told to bring you here and wait, so that's what we are doing. We're waiting. Now sit quietly and be a good girl." He pointed the gun at her face for added emphasis.

"Can you at least untie me?" she asked.

"Not yet, babe," he answered. "I'll do that later. Just sit tight and shut up."

There was a CB radio that was sitting on the desk in the office that began to squawk loudly and Paul got up from his chair and walked over to the receiver. He pushed the button and began to talk into CB.

"Go ahead, this is Red Man," he spoke into the handset. She listened closely to see if she could identify the voice.

"You get the package?" asked the person on the other side, a man with a deep voice.

"That's a 10-4. Package is delivered and ready, waiting your instructions. What's your 10-20?"

"I'll be back to you in about an hour or so. I need to make contact out here first and we'll see where we're headed after that."

"That's a big 10-4. We'll sit tight."

He was familiar enough with the CB that Jan figured her abductor was a person who had worked in trucking or had used one often. She became concerned when he turned back toward her with a gleeful look in his eye and bent down close to her.

"It's just you and me for a while sweetheart," he said. "Might as well get comfortable. I'll take those ties off you and give you a drink if you'll be good."

She nodded, and Paul moved over to her and loosed the ropes from her wrists. He handed her a canned Pepsi from the cooler he had nearby. He then went back to his chair and picked up the newspaper he had been reading and propped his feet on the desk. Jan decided that the best thing for her to do right now was to cause as few problems as possible and cooperate with this person. She knew that sooner or later someone would come looking for her, and she thought about Bryan and his promise to get in touch with her. She figured that if he didn't get an answer on her phone, he would go by the motel and figure out that something was wrong. She looked at her watch. It was 3:30, and they were supposed to meet at the restaurant where they had breakfast. She was convinced that they were already searching for her.

Chapter 27
Between Dayton and Chattanooga, same day

When it was clear he wouldn't be on time for lunch, Bryan decided to stop by a service station and use the pay phone to tell Jan they were running late. He let the phone ring several times to be sure that she wasn't in the bathroom or right outside her door, but there was no answer. They made another stop a few miles down the road at another pay phone and the result was the same.

"Jan must have gotten tied up, too," he told Joe. "Let's head over to her motel and see if she's there."

"Yeah, she's probably still tracking people down, man," answered Joe. "Let's head that way."

They arrived at Jan's motel at 4:30 and saw that her car was gone and that her drapes were pulled shut, so they assumed that she was either still working on something or she was with her parents. Before they left, they decided to stop by the office and see if anyone there had seen her leave or if she had left a message. They had no luck in either case.

On the drive over to their motel, they began discussing the situation.

"You know," began Bryan, "it's not like Jan to not call and leave word that she is going to be late."

"Well, Bryan," Joe responded, "we have been sort of out-of-pocket for the past few hours. Where would she call? Let's check with the front desk and see if she called our rooms. Then we'll contact her parents. She may be with them, or they may know where she is."

Bryan had an uneasy feeling after he checked with the motel front desk and was told that no one had called. He also talked to Jan's dad and was told that they had not seen their daughter since after the funeral service at about two. She'd told them that she was going to check on one more thing and then head back to meet with them at some restaurant. They asked to speak to Jan's mom, but he told them that she had gone out to take a walk when he had taken a shower and had not come back in yet.

After he hung up the phone, Joe told Bryan what had been said and they decided to head back to the motel and take a closer look. After arriving at the motel, they got the manager to unlock the door to Jan's room and they began to look around. Everything seemed to be in order, and nothing appeared out of place. As they were starting to leave, Bryan saw Jan's purse on the nightstand beside the bed and picked it up.

"I don't think Jan would have gone anywhere without this," he said as he dumped the contents of the purse out on the bed. "What do you see missing?"

"Well," answered Joe, "it's really strange that her wallet is here with her license and that her car keys are gone."

"Bingo," declared Bryan. "Somebody took Jan and her car."

"I'll call the Sheriff and have him put out an APB," said Joe as he picked up the desk phone and dialed the sheriff's office. "Here's the receipt from the rental car company with the car's tag number."

They instructed the manager not to let anyone in the room and to contact the sheriff's office if anyone showed or called. Then they climbed back into their car and made a speedy trip to the sheriff's office.

Purple Haze

Chapter 28
Chattanooga, July 10, 1970

Kathy walked quickly out of the hotel and out onto Broad Street and headed down the street to Loveman's Department Store. She was on her way to meet someone that she had no desire to see, but she was doing what she was told right now.

After her husband had gone to take a shower, the bedside phone had rung and this meeting was set up.

"Good afternoon, Kathy," the voice on the other end said.

"Who is this?" There was a fear in her voice as she sensed who was on the other end of the phone.

"You might say that this is someone from your past that you need to listen to very closely," he answered in a contemptuous tone.

She realized who she was talking with. "What do you want, Dan?" Almost reflexively, the volume of her voice had lowered, not wanting her husband showering in the next room to hear anything.

"Well, Kathy," he answered, "right now, I've got what I want. What I've always wanted, and if you ever want to see her again, you'll do exactly as I say."

"Okay, Dan, don't hurt Jan. I'll do whatever you say."

"I want you to leave your husband a note that you are going out for a walk. I want you to meet me at Loveman's department store right down the street in fifteen minutes."

"Where will you be?"

"I'll see you when you come in, and I'll make contact with you. It's very important for our daughter that you come alone and that you tell no one," he instructed her. "Do you understand that?"

"Yes, I understand. I will be there."

She wrote the note as instructed. Now she walked through the aisles looking ahead for Dan's face. When she entered the men's department, she felt a hand on her shoulder and a voice speaking softly from behind.

"Just act normal and don't call attention to us," he instructed her. "I'm going to lead you out the back door and we are going to take a little ride. Do you understand?"

"Yes."

He led her with his arm around her waist as they walked unnoticed through the back entrance and into his car which he had parked in a metered space. He opened the door for her, then he walked around the front of the car and climbed in opposite her. He was being very careful to make their actions appear casual and Kathy was responding well to his effort out of fear for her daughter. He turned the ignition, eased the car into the traffic on Market Street, and headed out of town.

"What do you want, Dan?" she demanded.

"What I want, I get," he answered. "Now just sit quiet and don't ask questions. You'll know soon enough."

"Where is Jan? You haven't hurt her, have you?"

"No," he answered. "She's okay for now; let's just hope we can keep her that way."

They drove in silence for the next twenty minutes. Kathy kept glancing out the window to remember where they were, should the need arise. Unfortunately, nothing at all looked familiar to her. They were headed out of town toward some old abandoned businesses and warehouses. She could see the river strobe through the trees. Soon, they entered a large area surrounded by a rusted fence and weeds growing up through the old parking lots. They pulled to the back of a large brick building and Kathy saw Jan's car parked near the door. She figured that Dan must have had someone else helping him, or else he'd have no way to get back to town. She had already figured out that Dan had killed Larry years ago and that he had buried him in the lake. She had kept her suspicions to herself because she had feared that bringing Dan into the story would make it necessary for her to confess to things that happened years ago while Larry was overseas. These were things that she had chosen to keep hidden. His obsession with her had been frightening, and she didn't want to revisit the time that had led up to her being forced to drop out of sight. She had actually feared for her life. Now it seemed she had become involved in something that she had no control over. For the safety of Jan, she was going to have to go along with whatever Dan had in mind for the time being.

After the car came to a stop in the back of the building next to Jan's rental car, Dan turned to her.

"As you will see, Kathy," he began in a soft voice, "we have Jan and she is safe. Nothing has happened to her and I, for one, plan to keep it that way. Now I need you to do exactly as you are told. Do we understand each other?"

"Yes, Dan," she answered. "I'll do whatever you say."

"Good girl, Kathy. Now when we get out of the car you stay with me and do not try to get away. Believe me, there is no place out here to go, and there is no one for miles around."

Dan took hold of her left arm and led her into the back of the warehouse and into the abandoned building. As they entered she saw some old yarn spools stacked to one side of the building in what looked to be a storage unit for a textile company. They walked down the dark building until they saw a light up ahead from what appeared to be an old office structure in the center. He motioned for her to sit on a stack of pallets and he took some rope from his jacket pocket and tied her to a nearby metal post.

"Now you sit here quietly," he ordered her, "and I will be right back."

After he tied her securely, he walked ahead to the office structure and disappeared inside.

As he entered, she could hear him talking to another man inside, and then she heard Jan's voice come from the inside of the building. Although she had been tied to a steel post, some fifty yards away from the office, the door to the office was ajar and the noise echoed through the empty warehouse. She listened quietly as Dan began to talk.

"Any problems?" Dan asked the man.

"Everything's been real quiet around here, man. She's been very cooperative."

Then Kathy heard Jan's voice.

"Is my mom out there?" her daughter asked the two men. By her tone, Kathy guessed that Jan was completely unaware of who Dan was, or what exactly was going on.

"We'll all get a chance for a reunion in a few moments, just sit tight," Dan told her in a gruff voice.

She could see the shadows of Dan and the other man in the windows but she could not see Jan, so she figured that she must have been tied in a chair or on the floor. After a few minutes, Dan came back through the door and walked toward her.

When Dan approached her, Kathy began pleading with him.

"Can I see Jan?" she asked. "I want to be sure that she's okay."

"She's fine, Kathy," said Dan. "I have no reason to hurt her."

"What do you want, Dan? What do you plan to do with us?"

"Well, I guess the answer to that question depends a lot on you, Kathy."

"What do you want from me, Dan? I have told no one about us, not even after all these years." Tears began to form in her eyes as she spoke. She continued, "If it's money you want, we can get that for you, just don't hurt us, please, Dan."

"What about what you did to me all those years ago, my dear? You don't think it hurt when I found out that you had left town and left no message or any explanation?"

"When I thought that Larry had been killed in the war, I just felt that nothing else was left for me."

"Do you remember that day at the post office in Chattanooga when you were expecting a letter from Larry, and you got all upset with me, and left in a hurry?" Dan asked as he looked down at her through the darkened space. "I found the letter you dropped while you were in a hurry to get away, and I made a decision then to remove Larry from the picture."

"Yes, Dan, I remember that day," she said as she lowered her head to avoid eye contact with him. "That was the day I decided to not see you again."

"So how did he wind up in the bottom of that lake? I don't understand," she asked him as he untied her hands from the post.

"There will be time to discuss that later, my dear. We will have plenty of time together." He took her by the arm and led her back outside toward the car. "Right now we have a phone call to make."

Chapter 29
Downtown Chattanooga, Same Day

After Bryan and Joe reached the sheriff's office, they discussed with him what they had and advised him to wait for a call from Jan's abductors. Bryan called Frank to see if he had been contacted yet and was surprised to discover that there had been no call.

"When was the last time you saw Kathy?" Bryan asked him.

"She left a note that she was going for a walk – I was taking a shower at the time so I can't be sure of the exact time, but I'd say an hour or more ago." Frank's voice began to show concern as they talked. "I know that sometimes when she goes shopping, she's gone for a couple of hours so I haven't been concerned. Do you think something has happened to her?"

"Do you remember anyone coming to the door?" asked Bryan.

"No, but I do remember hearing the phone ring."

"So that must be when she left. Whoever called her has probably kidnapped her and Jan. Jan's car is missing from the motel, and her purse and other stuff are still there," Bryan said. "Sit tight. We're coming over there in case there is a call from the abductors. Keep the phone off the hook until we get there. If they call, they will think the phone is busy and call back. We'll get there as soon as possible."

Bryan and Joe hurried out the door of the sheriff's office and left word at the desk with the sergeant on duty that they could be reached by radio and gave him the room number where Frank was waiting at the Read House. They headed toward downtown as quickly as the traffic would allow. Joe drove and Bryan sat quietly. Thoughts began to run through his head about the time that he and Jan had spent together. He settled on a song that they had heard at the music festival they had attended just a few days before:

Purple haze, all in my eyes,
Don't know if it's day or night.

Jimi Hendrix hit the nail right on the head. With all this suddenly spinning out of control, everything was really hazy. He began to worry about Jan and who had her, and what their intentions were.

"So, Bryan," began Joe. "Do you think this is the Bowers guy that's snatched the mother and daughter?"

"That's what I'm thinking," answered Bryan. "After we make contact with Frank and get things set up on the call, I think I'll go to the airport car rental agencies and see if we can get a handle on him. All we've got is that photo from his file and it's over thirty years old."

"It's a good idea, though, man. We might get lucky."

They parked in the front of the hotel, and rushed down the hall to Frank and Kathy's room.

"Hey, Frank, it's Bryan and Joe," Bryan said as he knocked. After the door opened, he continued. "Okay, Frank, hang the phone back up and let's see if we get a call."

"Maybe she wasn't kidnapped and just lost track of time. She's had a lot on her mind the past couple of days," said Frank.

"Yeah, it would be nice if she walked through the door in a few minutes, but that still wouldn't explain what happened to Jan." Joe walked over to the bureau where the phone was located and began to plan out their strategy. "I'm thinking that the call will come after dark and that's still an hour away. If the phone rings, you answer calmly, and make sure you tell him that you want to talk to Kathy to verify that she is okay and that he has her. I'll listen on the extension. Get as much information as he will give you."

"Why do you think it will be after dark?" asked Frank

"Well, if I was the kidnapper, I would want to be seen by as few people as possible, and the dark is better for that," Joe explained, thinking back to kidnapping cases he had handled in the past.

Joe was much more experienced with abductions than Bryan, since he had been with the Bureau for ten more years than Bryan, and had worked a couple of high profile kidnappings over the past few years. Bryan, although he was the more outgoing of the two, never questioned Joe's reasoning.

"Sure," answered Frank. "Should I ask about Jan?"

"No," answered Joe, "I'm sure he will tell you. We don't want him to know that you have contacted us, or that you even know about Jan." He turned to Bryan and told him to go to the airport to check the flight passenger lists and see if anyone from South Florida in that age group had come into the airport in the past couple of days. "Call me if you find anything," said Joe. "I'll hold things down here. While you're there, I'll call the sheriff and have him send a couple of his detectives over to the airport to help you go through the passenger manifests, that'll speed things up a little," suggested Joe.

"Will do," answered Bryan. "Also, ask him to send a couple of uniforms over to Jan's hotel to watch the Nova that the kidnapper left there. I'm not sure he'll come back for it, but you never know."

Bryan turned and walked out the door quickly, back down the elevator and into the waiting car at the front of the hotel. It took him about twenty minutes to arrive at the airport. He parked in front of the terminal and asked to see the security officer after he arrived. He was directed to an inner office behind the ticket counter area where he met the security chief.

The man in uniform held out his hand to greet Bryan. "I'm in charge of security here. What can I help you with?"

"I am looking for a person who possibly came into this airport within the last few days. The problem is," Bryan said, "he probably didn't use his real name and I have very few details about him, other than he came in from South Florida and is probably in his late fifties."

"Let's start with a name and see if he used that to book his flight."

"His real name is Dan Bowers," answered Bryan.

The security officer typed in the name and the dates for the expected flights. After a few minutes the teletype came back with an answer.

"No one with that name booked a flight into Chattanooga."

"Can we check with the connecting airlines and see if a flight was booked using that name to anywhere else during that time period?" asked Bryan.

"Sure thing," he answered, and he began to input the information. After a short wait, the officer was given a sheet with the information he needed.

"According to this teletype, there was a flight booked using that name two days ago from Miami to Houston," he reported to Bryan.

"I don't think he used that ticket. That was probably a diversionary booking in case anyone checked on him. Can we see the passenger list for flights from Miami to Chattanooga or Atlanta on that day? Maybe we can find him that way."

After a few minutes of waiting, a group of passenger lists began to be typed out and Bryan took the lists and began to look them over. He narrowed the lists first of all by focusing on passengers who were male and traveling alone. He eliminated most of the passengers and was left with a short list of ten males traveling alone that came into Chattanooga in the past three days. After he got his list together, he checked the profiles on the passengers and eliminated all those who were below the age of forty and he was left with only three names to check. There was a passenger named Dwight Powers who had traveled in two days ago from an Atlanta flight, one named Horace Green who had flown in three days ago on a straight through flight from Tampa, and another one named Tom Bradford, who had also flown in three days ago from Tampa. He eliminated the first name and began to concentrate on finding the whereabouts of the other two.

Neither person had rented a car from the airport, which meant that they either had someone meet them or they had a car waiting for them when they arrived. He gave one of the detectives at the airport with him the information he had on Horace Green, and told him to see if he could locate him as quickly as possible. He went to work on tracking Tom Bradford. After checking with local motels within reach of the airport, he had located information that a person using that credit card had checked in at the Ramada Inn near the airport. He hurried to his car and drove out to the Ramada and after identifying himself to the manager, he showed him a picture that he had of Dan Bowers and was told that a person who looked a lot like him had checked in a couple of nights ago. The manager gave him the check-in card that contained a license plate number and a car description. He gave him the key so that he could get into the room, but after searching the room, they found nothing. It was obvious that Dan had left and would not be returning.

When he returned to his car he got a radio call from the detective searching for Horace Green.

"Mr. Green is legit, Bryan," he began. "He is a sales rep for DuPont and was returning from a business trip in Tampa."

"I've found him," said Bryan. "The passenger who used the Tom Bradford alias is Bowers, and we need to get an APB on this vehicle as soon as possible." He gave the detective all the particulars on the car that Bowers had used when he checked in at the motel.

"Where are you headed now?" the detective asked. "We might need to get in touch with you quickly."

"I'm headed back to the hotel to see if anyone has called. I'll be in touch as soon as I get there. Call me on my radio or at the hotel."

It took Bryan a little less than thirty minutes to arrive back at the Reed House and up to the room. There had been no call and they were still awaiting the initial contact from Bowers. Bryan told them what he had discovered about the identity of the kidnapper.

"There was obviously something that happened between the two of them years ago after Kathy's husband was sent off to the war. I'm thinking that there may have been an affair between the two of them and when the husband returned, Bowers killed him and buried his body in the lake bed. It would fit the timeline with him working at the TVA site at the time and all the info we found out from the people who worked with him," Bryan said as he looked at his partner and Kathy's husband.

"So whatever happened was Dan Bower's secret," Bryan said. "Kathy had no idea that her husband had not come home."

"No, sir," replied Frank. "I'm positive that she thought he died at Pearl Harbor."

"If we look at all the evidence we have so far," added Joe, "with

Sam Daniels' death in particular, it looks like Bowers is trying to tie up some loose ends and I'm afraid this isn't going to be kidnapping for ransom. I'm thinking that this is a way to get the only connection to the murder that exists out of the picture."

"What about Jan?" asked Bryan. "If what you're saying is true, what motive would he have for kidnapping Jan?"

"I'm thinking," said Joe, "that Bowers believes that Jan is his daughter. That has to be it. Why else would he even bother to grab Jan?"

Purple Haze

Chapter 30
Off South Broad Street

Dan and Kathy had been driving for about an hour when Dan finally pulled the car into a parking spot near a pay phone at a strip mall off Broad Street. He took out a pair of handcuffs from the glove box and placed one end on Kathy's right wrist and the other end to the grab rail mounted on the inside of the front door, making it impossible for her to get out of the car. The parking lot was pretty well empty so it was not likely that she could get anyone's attention and that was why this particular lot was chosen.

"Now, Kathy," he reminded her, "your daughter is still with my buddy at the warehouse, so I wouldn't do anything to call attention to myself if I were you. If I don't return within a certain amount of time he has instructions to do whatever he wants to her, and I have a pretty good idea what that will be. So just be cool."

He closed the door and walked over to the pay phone. She watched him. After a few seconds, she noticed that Dan's face was beginning to turn red and she could see that he was very upset about something. He put the phone down on the metal shelf inside the booth and began walking back toward the car, obviously very upset.

He opened the door and climbed into the front seat and began to unlock her handcuffs. Something was obviously different than he wanted it to be, and Kathy was certain that Dan was close to reacting in a way she did not want him to react, so she moved cautiously and simply nodded her head as he gave her instructions. She had no intention of causing him any more stress at this time.

"Your husband wants to confirm that you are okay, so that is exactly what you are going to tell him." He pulled his gun out of his jacket and placed it against her side. "You are not to say anything out of the ordinary or it all ends sadly. Do you understand that, Kathy?"

She nodded helplessly, to reassure Dan that she would do whatever he told her to do. He walked around the front of the car and opened her door and reached in and took her elbow gently, and walked her over to the booth, walking close behind her, with the gun pressed against her ribs. He reached in and took the phone and began talking to Frank on the other end.

"Okay, here she is, now make it quick," he instructed him and then handed the phone to Kathy.

"Frank," she said, "it's me and I'm fine, just please do whatever he says."

Before she could say another word, Dan grabbed the phone and began to bark out his orders to Frank.

"Now," he said, "if you want to see her again as you last saw her, you will follow these instructions carefully. If I see a cop or anything goes wrong, this ends immediately. Believe me when I say this, because I really have nothing to lose here. Do you understand that?"

After a short pause, he began talking into the receiver again.

"I want you to call your bank in Nashville and I want them to wire one million dollars to this account within the next thirty minutes." He read off a long list of numbers to identify the account.

"After the money has been confirmed I will get back in touch with you, and let you know where you can pick up your wife." After a short pause, he continued, "By the way, your daughter is fine, too, and she will be released with your wife when the transaction is completed. Your thirty minutes begins right now," and he hung the phone up.

He took her by the elbow again and walked her back to the car, opened her door and let her in and then closed the door behind her. She watched him as he walked back in front of the car, and noticed as he took his time to observe what was going on around the car. He noted the traffic and cars that were suddenly coming and going in the drugstore parking lot. He took a cigarette out of his pocket coolly, lit it, and then got back into the driver's seat.

"So, what happens now?" she asked as he reentered the car.

"I take you back to the warehouse and then we wait and see if the money is deposited, then we'll take it from there," he answered.

They drove quietly back to the warehouse. Kathy was sure that Dan had no intention of ever releasing her, and she began to feel that her situation was hopeless. She worried about Jan and how she fit into all of Dan's plans. She was suddenly more concerned about her daughter than she was about herself. It was doubtful whether Dan felt any closeness to his daughter--she felt that she needed to make a play on Dan's emotions and try to buy some time for herself and for Jan. If there was time, maybe she could be found and this would all end. She decided that the time would come for her to make that play, but for the time being, the best thing was to cause as little trouble as possible.

After a few minutes they turned off the main road, back through the old fenced-in property and toward the warehouse. It seemed to be such a deserted place, there was very little hope that they could be found. She sat quietly as the car stopped, and then followed Dan back into the warehouse after he released her from the handcuffs.

She was led into the room where Jan was being held and Dan motioned for her to sit on the mattress on the floor next to her daughter. Paul had already moved Jan from the office to one of the two small rooms where he had placed the mattresses. She took Jan's hand and nodded to her that everything was okay, and Dan shut the door behind the two of them and disappeared from sight. They sat close together and held each other tightly and said nothing. They just needed to be together right now; there would be time to talk later.

Dan went back out into the office area where Paul was to discuss their progress.

"I'm going back out to confirm that the money has been transferred, so I should be gone about thirty minutes to an hour," he instructed Paul. "Just sit here and keep an eye on them until I get back."

Dan turned and walked out the door.

Chapter 31
Read House Hotel

After Frank hung up the phone, he turned and looked at Bryan, who had listened in on the conversation on the other phone. There was a dejected look on his face as he began to talk about the demands.

"There's no problem with the money, my bank will back me up on it based on my property and on my company," he said to Bryan and Joe. "I'm just afraid that after I make that transfer, this guy will disappear and I'll never see Kathy and Jan again."

"It's obvious that he has put a lot of thought into this," Joe answered. "The car he picked up at the airport was registered to a company in Memphis owned by his son. The bogus name he used on the tickets and at the motel, and no return flight booked. There are a lot of things we need to tie up pretty quickly."

"First of all," said Bryan, "let's get the wire transfer done, and then we'll try to figure out our next move." He took out a small note pad and began to write as he spoke. "Also, Frank, when you call your bank get a locale on the bank that matches that account number. That'll help us determine where they're headed next."

Frank walked over to the chest of drawers and took out a black book, turned the pages and located the number of his banker and began placing the call. He gave the bank official the account number and asked him to locate where the money was being deposited, and was placed on hold while it was looked up. After a short wait, he was told that the transfer had been completed and that it went to Houston Bank and Trust in Texas.

"Chances are he is not planning to drive that far, so he must be flying out of here or an airport close by," said Joe. "I'll contact Atlanta and Knoxville and give them the bogus name and description and tell them to be on the lookout."

"Good idea, Joe," added Bryan. "You might call Nashville, too. We've got a tag number the car from the airport parking lot attendant, and a fairly good description of both him and the car. Also, he'll have the two women with him. That is, of course, unless he lives up to his bargain and releases them."

"But he promised me that they would be released if I transferred the money, I certainly hope he does as he said he would." Frank was obviously upset with the logic of the two agents.

"Well, we certainly hope that happens but we have to assume that he will not and then try to figure out his next move," Joe answered as he sat down next to Frank. "You've done all that he asked you to do, now we hope that he does what he is supposed to do."

Bryan moved over toward the two men as they were talking, and looked out the window to the street below as he talked. "This guy doesn't seem to be your normal kidnap-for-ransom guy. I'm thinking that this guy is more into possession and taking back what he thinks he lost years ago." He turned to face them as he finished his summation, "I hope that I am wrong and he releases them."

Bryan and Joe decided that they would go to the regional office and work from there so they could have easier access to information as it became available to them. They told Frank to sit tight and let them know if they heard anything at all from the kidnapper or anything else that could be related to the case.

"Couldn't I go with you guys to your office?" he pleaded as they got ready to leave.

"I really think you need to stay here by the phone in case he calls back or if Kathy needs to call you," answered Joe. "He might stick to his word and release them and they will call here. Just let us know as soon as he does. Call this number." He handed Frank a card with the regional office number on it.

On the way down in the elevator, Bryan expressed his concern to Joe about the events of the past hour. Neither of them seemed convinced that there was going to be a release, and they both felt that the best strategy was to continue a search for the car.

"I'll get on the phones and call the three nearby airports with the info we have," said Joe.

"And I'll work with the bank where the money was deposited," added Bryan, "and go backward from there. There may be some connection with the Houston bank and Bowers' son, Billy."

They got back into the car and drove back to the offices, and then ran into the building to get to work on making some calls. Joe went to an open cubicle and began making calls to the airports. Each of the airport's security office was given the tag number and description of the car and a description of Dan Bowers and of the hostages. He also faxed the descriptions and the photos to each security office.

While he was working on that end of the investigation, Bryan called the bank in Houston that matched the account number. He finally got in touch with the bank's president, who gave him the information he needed on the account.

"The account is listed as the New Era Construction Company in

Houston," the bank officer told Bryan. "According to the account information, it's a company headquartered in Memphis, but they're building an office complex downtown here."

"Is there a name associated with the account?" asked Bryan.

"Well, according to the records here, the company is registered under the name William Bowers and there are a couple of names authorized for the account locally."

"Give me those names and addresses," said Bryan.

"David Windsor is listed as the site coordinator," said the bank president, "and there is a Grace Watkins on the account as well."

"We need to know immediately if there is any activity in the account that involves that million dollar deposit," instructed Bryan. "There is probably going to be a huge withdrawal later today. Let me know quickly."

"Yes, sir," he answered. "We sure will."

After he hung up the phone, he called the regional office in Houston and gave them the information on Windsor and Watkins, and asked that someone be assigned to watch them both. He gave them the address of the office complex and their local addresses and phone numbers that the bank president provided.

He then called the office in Memphis to coordinate an investigation of Bowers' son, Billy, and to send someone over to question him in relation to the whereabouts of his father.

"It's very important that we know why a car registered to him ended up at the airport in Chattanooga and what knowledge he has of the kidnapping," he instructed the agent in Memphis. "I know that he and his dad have been in touch and I'm certain that he knows what is going on. Why don't you have someone check the phone records, too, and see if there are any calls to or from Chattanooga?"

"Will do," answered the Memphis agent. "Should I call you back at this number?"

"Yeah," answered Bryan. "I need the info as soon as possible."

He hung up the phone, about to walk over toward Joe's desk, when the front desk secretary came back and told him that the Sheriff's office had called. They spotted the car that Bowers had used from the airport.

"Transfer the call to my desk," he instructed her.

The phone rang once and he picked it up.

"This is Inspector Langston," answered Bryan.

"This is Deputy Morgan with the Hamilton County Sheriff's Department. We were told to call you as soon as we got a location on the vehicle you put in the APB for."

"Yes, sir, Deputy Morgan," answered Bryan. "Where is the car?"

"The car was spotted about five minutes ago on Highway 11 north headed out of the city. We are in observation of the car."

"Okay, my partner and I are headed that way, I'll keep in touch by radio."

"Head north out of town through the Brainerd area, that's where the vehicle is at this moment, but the car is headed toward the airport."

"Just stay with him and let us know if he stops or changes directions. We'll head straight to the airport."

He hung up the phone and ran over to Joe's desk where he was making phone calls and told him what was going on. The two of them dashed to the car, and headed south out of town toward the airport.

Purple Haze

Chapter 32
Off South Broad

Kathy knew that she had very little time to talk to her daughter, and she wanted to take the time they did have to plan their strategy. She felt that Dan planned on separating them and that they would be going in opposite directions.

"Look, Jan," she began, in a calm, reassuring voice, "I know that Dan has made a ransom demand and that he told Frank that he planned to release us when the money was dropped."

"So there's going to be a money exchange for us?" she asked. The fear was evident in her words.

"No," answered Kathy calmly. "The money was deposited into a bank account somewhere, so there's not going to be an exchange."

"So how's it supposed to go down?"

"He told Frank that as soon as the money was confirmed, he would release us both," answered Kathy, "but that's not what is going to happen."

"What do you think is going to happen, Mom?"

"There're two of them and two cars," Kathy replied. "I'm certain they are going to split us up and go in opposite directions out of here. They probably have a designated spot to meet up later and two different ways to get there, but I have no idea where or when."

"I feel like we've got to try and remember all we can," Jan said to her mom. "If they catch one of the cars out of here, it'll help if we can remember all we can about the other person who is not with us. Try to get the tag number of the other car when we get out of here and a description so it will help them find it."

Kathy held Jan tightly and they spent the next few minutes in a reassuring hug that everything was going to work out. They both had a chance to analyze their situation and they realized that there was no escape, and that their hopes were small. It was easy for Jan to remember how her mom had always gotten her out of tough spots. This was still her mom, and she believed in her.

"That sounds like a good plan. Just remember that I love you, Jan and we're going to get through this." She took her daughter's hand and squeezed it hard. "Think positive thoughts and try not to worry about me. Just take care of yourself, and we'll get through this together."

By the time they had finished talking, Dan Bowers walked into the room with the man who had kidnapped Jan. Dan walked over to the two of them, reached down and lifted Jan by the arm. He did not look at Kathy, and began talking directly to Jan.

"Okay," he began, "this is what is going down."

He looked at both of them, Jan flailing helplessly in his right hand and Kathy looking up at them from the mattress, his eyes steely with determination so that there was no mistaking his intentions.

"Now, you follow directions exactly as you are told and don't cause any problems," he said to them.

Then he pulled Jan's wrist forcefully to remove her from her mother's side. "You go with him," he said to Jan, pointing to his partner, "and don't do anything to call attention to yourself or it will end soon for you and your mother. Do you understand that?"

"Yes," she answered. "I'll do exactly as you say."

Dan handed her over to Paul and handed him the keys to the car that he picked up at the airport.

"So, I'm taking this car?" Paul asked.

"Yeah, I need the keys to her rental. If they have a description of me it won't fit with you." Dan deliberately withheld his true intentions from Paul and decided to send him in the opposite direction as a decoy. "Put her in the trunk and keep her out of sight. I want you to drive out of town and go north to Cleveland. There's a small airport there right off Highway 11 and we'll meet you there."

"So you're gonna be right behind me out of here?"

"We're leaving about fifteen minutes later," he said, almost dismissively. "Should be there in about an hour," he added, but then he took Paul just outside the door and whispered into his ear.

"As soon as you get clear of town, pull off the road somewhere and dispose of your baggage. It wouldn't be good if they pulled you over and she was in the trunk."

Paul grabbed Jan's arm roughly and led her outside the warehouse out to the parking lot. She was careful to get a final look at the rental car and made a mental note of the tag number. Paul took her over to the Cutlass and motioned for her to get into the trunk. She began to pull against him even though she knew there was nowhere to go. With the back of his hand he hit her on the side of the face and reminded her of her hopelessness. After the slap, she once again went limp and Paul was able to handle her with ease. She laid in a fetal position at the base of the trunk and Paul tied her hands and feet together so she could move very little. He closed the trunk and entered the car and cranked the engine. Jan was frightened by the darkness that surrounded her and became nauseous as the exhaust fumes entered the trunk. She tried to

225

hold her breath as much as possible to avoid inhaling the sickening odor. She tried to count to herself the turns and stops out of the warehouse site, but she became so concerned with fighting the fumes that her immediate survival became primary to her.

She could hear the music from the radio that Paul was listening to and she felt the road smooth out as the car picked up speed and headed out of town. Paul was obviously driving with the A/C on, and the windows rolled up so that he could hear the noises that she made in the trunk.

He planned on driving through the city and out into a little town called Ooltewah where he knew of a spot he could deposit the "baggage" in the trunk. It was still early evening, so she noticed that the traffic was still quite heavy, and that there was a lot of stopping and starting.

Some distance behind them, Bryan and Joe were now closing in pursuit of the chase vehicles and Bryan radioed to the sheriff's car ahead.

"This is Agent Langston," Bryan said into the radio. "Do you have a ten-twenty on the Cutlass?"

"That's ten-four, Agent Langston," answered Deputy Morgan. "The vehicle is two cars in front of us right now."

"You got other cars nearby?"

"Roger," he answered, "there are two other vehicles ahead in front of the Cutlass."

"Copy that," said Bryan.

"What do you want us to do, sir?" asked Deputy Morgan.

"Let's give him a siren and some lights and see if we can get him stopped," instructed Bryan. "Tell your officers that there is a hostage in the car with the suspect and not to endanger her. If she's not in the car visually, he may have her in the trunk."

"That's a 10-4. I'll pass that on to the other cars."

"We need to take this guy alive if we can, Deputy."

He turned on his roof lights and sounded the siren as he moved in behind the Cutlass. As expected, the Cutlass began to speed up and weave in and out of traffic. Right after he passed a busy intersection on Brainerd Road, he made a sharp left across traffic into an industrial area. The three sheriff cars and the FBI car with Joe and Bryan followed him as he sped into the group of factories and warehouses.

Jan had been in the trunk for about thirty minutes when she felt the Cutlass suddenly pick up speed. She found herself bouncing around helplessly as the car began to take turns sharply and suddenly. It seemed like she was bouncing even more as the car crossed railroad tracks and over rough pavement. She grabbed hold of the mats on the floor of the trunk to cushion herself against the sides of the trunk, but she was jolted against the front of the trunk as the car seemed to crash into something in its path. She began to fear that the car would burst into flames and began to move around as much as possible and try to free her ropes. It was impossible. Her kidnapper had tied them too well and too tight. She heard the driver's door open, and she began to fear fire even more. Gunshots went off outside the car and she flinched. The shots were loud and ricocheted as they hit the car. What if a stray shot penetrated the trunk lid? She tried to kick the car as much as possible to call attention to herself, but was unable to move very much.

Suddenly the shooting stopped, and the sounds changed to voices approaching the car. She recognized Bryan's voice and began to call out his name through the gag that was bound around her mouth. The trunk lid opened and there stood Bryan, the most beautiful sight she could imagine! He helped her out of the trunk, took off the ropes and the gag and held her shaking body closely to his. She knew that she had come very close to death and when she looked at the bullet-riddled body of her abductor and the condition of the car, she was filled with relief that she had escaped alive.

"It's all right, Jan," he said. "We got him."

The car had hit a concrete abutment and was surrounded by police cars with flashing lights whirling. It was a great sight for Jan to see, but she knew that her mother was still in danger and that she had to help them find her.

"What do you know about your mom and Bowers?" Bryan asked her. "Do you have any idea where they might be headed or anything else that can help us?"

"I think I could find the place where they held us," she answered. "I'll tell you what else I've got on the way there."

Joe got into the driver's seat with Bryan in the front on the passenger side. Jan sat in the back and began to talk as the car moved forward.

She gave a description of the car and the tag number to Joe and told them that she felt that they were going in the opposite direction. Bryan wrote down the information in his note pad as Jan talked.

"I kind of got the feeling that he expected this to happen and felt like he would have a better chance of getting out of here if he sent his partner out as a sacrificial lamb. I overheard him say something to his partner about a plane in Cleveland, but I don't really think that's where he's headed," Jan said.

"Let me get this APB out now so they can start looking for the vehicle," said Bryan. "He's already got a thirty-minute head start." He got on the radio and called in the tag number and a description of the car. He told the voice on the other end that he was headed back to the crime site and that he would be in touch.

"You got a couple of calls back here," said his secretary into the radio. "Do you want me to give them to you now or are you coming by here?"

"Tell you what, Gail," he said, "give them to me now."

"You got a call back from the bank in Houston and they said that there had been a person come by and make a withdrawal on the account you checked on."

"Did he get a name for me?"

"Yeah, he did," Gail answered. "It was a Grace Watkins. She took the money and left the bank about ten minutes ago."

"Okay, Gail," he instructed. "Call the Houston office and find out if they have a tail on her, and tell them to stay close to her. Follow the money."

"Will do, Bryan," said Gail. She paused, then continued, "The other call was from the Memphis office. He said that Billy Bowers was in his plane and headed to Atlanta, Georgia."

"Chances are he'll land somewhere before he gets there." Joe said to Bryan, and asked for the radio and gave Gail some further instructions. "Call the other airports between Chattanooga and Atlanta and give them a description of the plane and the number. He'll probably land in Dalton, Rome, or maybe Marietta. Call those first. Let us know if you hear anything."

"Listen, Gail," said Joe. "We're headed over to the place where the hostages were held. We're hoping to find something there. I'll have my radio with me, so call me when you hear anything."

He signed off, and hung up the radio and as he did, Jan began to think about where she had been and began to talk to Bryan about some of the familiar things she noticed as she was being driven to the kidnap spot the first time.

"Bryan," she began, "do you remember that day we drove up the mountain?"

"Sure," he answered. "Did something look familiar there?"

"When we drove there right after he grabbed me, I remember passing the turnoff where we went up Lookout Mountain."

They headed toward Broad Street and took the turnoff from the downtown connector that pointed toward Lookout Mountain. As they passed the buildings she began to recognize familiar sites and directed them around the river at the base of the mountain.

"We went this way," she instructed and pointed straight ahead under a small underpass toward the town of St. Elmo. "I remember going through that underpass, and we went just a short distance until the road narrowed. It seems like it should be right about in this area."

"What exactly are we looking for here, Jan?" asked Joe as he drove the car slowly.

"I remember a high chain link fence, sort of rusted, and it had a gate--a big, double gate with a rusty looking, white sign on it."

She looked intently to the right and spotted what she thought could be the gate.

"That's it—right there," she said, pointing to her right. "Drive right through there, I'm sure this is it. But I thought it was on the river over there."

"You probably saw the creek in the back of the property. It runs into the river where we just drove past. This looks like an old abandoned warehouse."

As Joe drove through the gate, Bryan looked through his notes and spotted a note about the property that he had gotten from the records office when he was checking on property owned by Billy

Bowers. He shared the news with Joe and Jan.

"This property *is* owned by Billy Bowers," Bryan said. "This has to be the place."

"Oh, yeah," said Jan. "This is definitely it."

"Looks like they're long gone," Bryan said. "Let's go in and see if we can find anything he might have left behind to give us an idea as to where they are headed."

He parked the car in front of the same door that Jan remembered, and she led them into the area where they had been held, then into the room next to it where the two men had been talking. They found nothing that would help them, and so they returned to the car and radioed the location to the sheriff's department. He told them that they were at the warehouse and that they could find nothing to help them. While they were talking, a call came in to the sheriff's office giving the location of an abandoned car that fit the description he had given them earlier.

The location was about five or six miles from where they were, so he told the dispatcher that they were headed that way. They went south on U.S. 41 to the location and found a group of patrol cars, lights flashing, in the parking lot of a Krystal hamburger restaurant. The building was located in front of a motel complex and next to an office building.

"Are there any cars missing from here?" Joe asked the deputy as he walked over to him.

"There haven't been any so far. We're still hoping to get a tag number for the car they may be in now."

There was very little chance now of knowing what car they were in and where they were headed. Until more information came in, they were going to have to rely on their instincts and hope that they guessed right. Since the car had been found on U.S. 41 headed south out of town, Bryan concluded they must be headed toward Atlanta. Most of that route was open interstate, but a portion was still under construction. It wasn't likely that they would do anything to call attention to themselves, and they weren't even sure if Kathy was in the car or trunk. In fact, they did not know whether they were looking for a single male or a couple, and even if they did, there was little if any chance of apprehension.

As they got back into the car and were driving south on U.S. 41, a call came in on the radio from the FBI office. Gail told them that a flight plan had been filed on Billy Bower's plane and that he was planning to land in Rome, Georgia.

"According to the flight plan, the plane should be on the ground there now," Gail told them. "No flight plan has been filed on the plane after that."

"Okay," said Joe into the radio. "Chances are that's where he is headed. Call ahead to the sheriff's department in Floyd County and give them the number on the plane and see if they can work it from that end. We're never going to get there in time."

"That's a 10-4, Joe," answered Gail. "Will do."

Bryan looked at the atlas in the car and saw that they were still thirty-five or forty minutes out from the airport. Chances were pretty good that Bowers was probably close to the airport by now. Their only hope was that the Floyd County Sheriff could hold them up until they got there.

"Mom told me that he was likely to try to get off the radar as soon as possible," Jan said from the back seat. "She told me that he was desperate and would likely take a lot of chances."

"She had that figured right," agreed Bryan. "With all he's got hanging over his head, he'll probably try to leave the country."

Purple Haze

Chapter 33
U.S. 27 South, 1970

From Dan's point-of-view, everything was going according to plan. In the warehouse, he'd decided that escaping with Kathy meant more to him than building a relationship with a daughter who had never known him. Sending Paul in the Cutlass with Jan created enough of a diversion to allow him to get away with Kathy. She was his.

He had arranged ahead of time for Billy to have the plane in Rome in enough time for him to get there and get out, before they could catch up with him. Switching the cars bought him even more time since they had no idea what car he was in or where he was headed. His plan was to fly out of Rome to Shreveport, Louisiana, where he was to meet up with Billy's girlfriend, Grace. They were cruising down U.S. 27 South toward Rome without a cop in sight. They were only a few minutes away from the airport, when he saw a sheriff's car up ahead traveling in the same direction with its roof lights flashing and twirling. He had told Billy to be prepared in case they showed up at the airport before him. As he neared the airport, he saw another sheriff's car coming from the opposite direction, this time with lights and siren. Still, he felt confident that they did not have anything yet on the car he was driving so they would not be looking for him in it. It was likely that the FBI had traced Billy's plane to the airport, and that's why they were here.

He turned in his seat and got the automatic rifle and the pistol that he had lying next to him covered with a blanket. He threw the blanket in the back seat and began to speak to his unwilling passenger sitting next to the window.

"There's fixing to be some real trouble up ahead," he began, "so I'd keep my head down if I were you."

She obediently got on her knees with her head facing in the opposite direction lying on the seat, out of view and out of danger. She was sure there would be bullets flying everywhere, and she was scared beyond belief.

As he entered the gate to the airport, he could hear the shooting from the hangar. He rolled down the driver's side window and placed the automatic rifle through the opening. Billy appeared to be inside the hangar, and he looked like he had at least one person with him. As he neared the hangar, he made a sharp turn which left him facing the side of one of the deputy cars. He began to shoot a series of shots into the side of the car and the door to the deputy's car swung open and a confused deputy walked into the line of fire and was cut down. The other car, which was facing into the hangar, had been shot several times by the gunfire and it appeared that all inside the car were dead. As far as Dan knew, that left only one deputy, the driver of the car he was shooting at. He decided to go straight at the other car, so he turned his wheels sharply and drove straight at the deputy's car. The deputy dropped his car in reverse and tried to avoid a collision, and as Dan's car drove toward him, Dan fired a stream of bullets from his revolver that he had picked up from the seat beside him after he laid the empty rifle next to his leg. The bullets shot out the back window of the patrol car and the driver forced the wheel hard left roaring past Dan and the car backed into the gas pump and burst into flames.

"I think that's it," he said to Kathy. "You can come up now. Looks like we got them all. Let's head over there," he said pointing inside the hangar.

As they drove into the hangar, they passed the bullet-ridden deputy's car and the body of one of the deputies on the concrete next to the car. The other deputy was still in the car and appeared to be dead. He saw Billy and his partner as they came from behind a rack of equipment and began to wave to him.

"Hey, Dad," yelled one of the men, as he waved his automatic rifle in the air.

Kathy looked at the young man who stood about six foot two and looked to be in pretty good physical shape. He looked a lot like his dad and Kathy thought about how much he looked like Dan the last time she had seen Billy prior to this encounter with him. He looked to be in his late thirties which would have been about right, since he was six the last time Kathy had seen him.

"Let's go, Pop," he yelled, and made a sweeping motion with his rifle over his head to indicate that the plane was ready in the rear of the hangar.

"All right, Kathy," ordered Dan. "Head over toward the plane and don't cause any trouble. I'll be right behind you."

Kathy did exactly as commanded and moved quickly from the car toward the Cessna that was idling straight ahead. She moved over to the plane and Billy helped her as she stepped up into the cockpit of the plane. He motioned her to sit in the back and she settled down on the leather seat on the passenger side of the plane. Dan entered the plane and sat on the passenger front seat and Billy's partner sat next to her in the back of the plane. Billy was the last to enter, after he removed the chocks from the wheels, and sat down in the pilot seat. He quickly began to maneuver the plane out of the hangar and rolled down the runway to prepare for a takeoff. Kathy could feel the engine of the plane as it increased RPMs and she felt the surge as the plane began to pick up speed down the runway and then the lift as it left the runway and became airborne. Just as the plane left the ground, she could see the blue lights of more police cars arriving at the airport, but they were too late to help her. A feeling of doom swept over Kathy as she sat quietly in the seat and looked out the window and wondered how this was all going to end.

"Man!" said Billy excitedly. "That was like the old movies we used to watch together when I was a kid. Just as it looked like things were going to hell, in rides the cavalry to the rescue with their guns a-blazing."

Dan remembered that Billy had always loved excitement but he also remembered how his mother always tried to keep him away from guns. Billy always had other people to do this kind of thing for him, and suddenly doing it himself created a real rush.

"Yeah, that was a little close," answered Dan. "What's the plan, Billy?"

"I got a call back from Grace in Houston, and she picked up the money for you and gave me a location to meet her in Shreveport."

"So, you have a car to meet us?" asked Dan.

"No, but I've got a car waiting there that we can use."

"Look, Billy," said Dan, "you've stuck your neck out enough on this thing, why don't you just give me the details, and you take off back to Houston or Memphis after you drop us off." He paused for a moment and looked at his son, then continued, "I really didn't mean to involve you this much in this deal."

"Well, Dad," he answered, "it looks like I *am* involved, so we're in this together for the long haul." He paused for a moment then looked at Dan and continued, "I've got a good way of getting us out of the country, but we've got to get to Brownsville, Texas, to make the connection across the border. After we land, we'll meet Grace and make two runs to Brownsville. You can take the car, and I'll drive there in another with Grace and meet you somewhere."

"That sounds good," said Dan.

"So, we're going to Mexico?" asked Billy.

"We're heading there first," answered Dan, "on the way to Costa Rica. I've purchased some land with a house close to the Pacific coast. I'm planning on setting up a fishing charter business."

"Costa Rica, huh? That sounds like a great place to drop out of sight."

"Well, we've got to meet up with your girlfriend and go from there."

Kathy listened to the conversation going on between the two of them and tried to relax as much as possible in the back seat. She knew that the police were on the trail of her abductor, and she prayed that they would figure out where they were heading. She thought to herself that maybe the best connection would be from the other end. If they could figure out where they were heading, they could stop this thing before Dan made it across the border into Mexico. She knew that afterwards, her chances were slim to none.

"Oh, by the way," said Billy, pointing to the man sitting in the back seat, "this is B.J. After we land, he's going to fuel the plane up and head her back to Memphis."

Dan nodded to B.J. "Nice to meet you."

They had been in the air for about an hour and Dan turned around in his seat to check on Kathy.

"You comfy back there?" he asked her

"About as comfortable as I can be under the circumstances," she answered.

"Billy's changed a lot since you saw him last, huh?"

"Yeah," she answered, "he looks and acts a whole lot more like his daddy than he did the last time I saw him."

Dan glared at her after her statement, then turned round and talked with Billy.

"What are you planning on doing when all this is over?" Dan asked Billy.

"Well," he answered, "when B.J. takes the plane back, I'm sure the cops are going to be all over him with questions about me. We've got his story worked out that he flew me to Atlanta to meet a developer from Mexico and I flew with him to look over some property he had near Mexico City. So, we're going to spend a couple of weeks down there before we head back to Memphis. By then, everything will have been confirmed with my friend in Mexico City, and it'll be a done deal."

"Sounds like you've got it all worked out," said Dan.

"The only people that can put me at that airport in Rome are dead. Doubt they'll be talking much."

"What about Grace?" asked Dan. "How reliable is she?"

"She's the best there is for this, believe me. She knows what she is doing."

"And she picked up the money?"

"When I talked to her after I landed in Rome," answered Billy, "she had the money and there was no one following her."

Dan seemed content and laid his head back against the back of the seat and dozed off. He was awakened by the sound of the landing gear engaging and he looked out his window at the sleepy town of Shreveport, Louisiana. He was almost home free.

Purple Haze

Chapter 34
Rome, Georgia

Joe and Bryan were thirty minutes from the airport when they received word of the gunfight at the hangar. They were told that there were four dead officers on the site, and that Dan Bowers had already taken off in a plane bound for an unknown destination. When they arrived, they saw the two deputy cars that were riddled with bullet holes and a car that they did not recognize, and realized that it was the car that Dan Bowers had stolen in Chattanooga. They looked over the car and found nothing that told them anything about where they were headed. There was no one left alive at the airport that could have given them any information about where their plane was headed. Bryan was perplexed about which way to look next when Jan volunteered some valuable insight as to where they might be headed.

"I remember Dan telling someone on the phone that they would meet them in Shreveport," she said, struggling to recall all the facts. "Seems like I heard a woman's name, like maybe Gloria or Grace, or something like that."

"Had to be Grace," said Bryan. "That was the name of the contact person we were tailing in Houston. I'll call our man there and see if they have anything on her."

He ran into the small office at the airport and made a quick call then returned in a few minutes with the news. "According to our agent in Houston, Grace left the city about three hours ago and drove to Shreveport. He said that she drove to a small airstrip just north of town and that they were watching her but that, so far, she has not contacted anyone."

"Maybe they are going to spend the night there and drive out in the morning," said Joe. "Let's get on the road and head to Shreveport."

"We'll never make it there," said Bryan. "We'll use one of these planes and fly there. I've got a recreational pilot license, to fly any plane of 180 horsepower or smaller with four or less seats, like that one over there," he said pointing to a small Piper Cub.

As Bryan turned to walk toward the office to make arrangements, he spoke to Joe. "Get back on the phone and talk to Agent Huddleston in the Houston office. Make sure he has the agent on Grace Watkins to keep up with her and let us know where they go. Tell him to have the agent meet us at the airport in a couple of hours. We'll be flying out within the next thirty minutes."

Jan put her hand in Bryan's and looked into his eyes and asked if she could go with them. "I really need to go," she pleaded. "I can't stay here and worry about everything going on down there."

"It's going to be very dangerous," he answered. "I'd rather you stayed here and let us keep you informed."

"Look, Bryan," she argued, "it can't be any worse than what I've been through the past twelve hours."

"Okay Jan, you're right. But you have to promise me that you're going to stay out of the way and not interfere."

"I promise," she said and hugged his neck in gratitude.

Bryan went into the hangar to see if he could locate the keys to one of the planes he was certified to fly. After searching through the office, he found a set of keys for a Cessna 172I, built in 1968, and the flight records on the plane showed that it was full of fuel and ready to fly. As he went behind the desk to get the keys, he saw the body of the airport flight controller lying in a pool of blood. He yelled outside for one of the deputies and continued to search for information on the plane. He read the material that was attached to the records and found that the plane was owned by a person in Rome, so he picked up the phone, identified himself, and told the man on the other end that he was going to use the plane and explained the emergency to him. After he assured the gentleman that he was a certified pilot and that the FBI would assure the safe return of his plane, the man gave the okay for the plane to be used. Because he found the plane on the outside of the hangar, it had been far away from the gunfire and there was no damage to it anywhere. He walked around the plane and did all the visual checks, removed the chocks from the wheels and climbed into the cockpit. Since the tower in Rome was not operational, he contacted the tower in nearby Cartersville to file his flight plan and to receive instructions. While he was waiting for a reply, he read through the manual and discovered that the plane cruised at a speed of 130 mph. Knowing that Shreveport was roughly 550 air miles away, he figured a four-hour flight ahead. He wasn't sure how much of a head start they had, but it was surely an hour or more. Since it was now 6:15 p.m., he estimated landing time in Shreveport for nine thirty CST on the conservative side.

After he cleared the hangar and started to enter the taxiway, he stopped and picked up Jan and Joe who were waiting at the edge for him. Joe opened the door for Jan and she climbed into the back seat on the pilot side and he entered the front seat next to Bryan. As he did, he began to talk about his phone call.

"I talked to the Houston office and Agent Huddleston said that the Watkins woman had stopped by a bank on her way out of town and came out with a briefcase full of money. She got into the car and drove non-stop to the airfield in Shreveport and that is where she was at the time I talked with her."

"Was there anyone else there, besides the airport personnel?" asked Bryan.

"No," he answered, "it was just her. The agent on the scene said that there was a car there that no one seemed able to identify. According to a guy in the hangar, someone came by yesterday and left the car and drove off with a guy in a dark green pickup."

"What instructions did you leave for the guy at the airport?" he asked as he taxied the plane for takeoff.

"I told him to stay with the guy with the hostage and to get someone else there to follow the other car."

"Sounds good, man," said Bryan as the plane left the ground and they were skyward, on their way to Shreveport.

Jan and Joe both became quiet and were soon dozing away the miles. Bryan concentrated on the cockpit, reading the dials and making sure of his coordinates. He was flying visually for the most part and used the newly opened Interstate 20 that ran from beyond Atlanta westward all the way through most of Texas. Although there were stretches of it still incomplete, the route was easy to follow and he used identifiable towns and cities as markers. He was able to identify the town of Tuscaloosa by the University of Alabama campus in the center of the city, and headed southwest to Jackson, the next major city on the route.

After a couple of hours, Jan began to stir and talk to Bryan.

"Where are we?" she asked. "I'm sorry I dozed off, I should have stayed awake and helped you."

"Well," answered Bryan, "only one person can sit here and fly. We're getting close to Jackson, Mississippi. You can help me by seeing if you can locate the capitol building downtown."

After a few minutes, the downtown lights of Jackson appeared out the window and although it was too dark to actually locate the capitol building, the center of the city was rather obvious. From there, Bryan set a course for south/southwest that would take him close to Shreveport. After he crossed the Mississippi River, he followed I-20 due west and later saw the lights of a city that appeared to be Shreveport. He radioed the tower for landing, but they told him that it was Monroe and he needed to go another thirty minutes west to get to Shreveport. Finally, the city came into view and he radioed the tower for instructions. His landing was a little bouncy, but not bad for someone who had not flown in several months.

When they landed the plane, they headed for the hangar at the end of the runway and a dark blue sedan awaited them as they disembarked. A rather short but well-built young man in a short-sleeved white shirt walked up to them and introduced himself as Agent Harris. He told them that the plane had landed there about two hours ago and that one of the men in the plane refueled the plane and took off again alone. He said he checked with the tower and the pilot had filed a flight plan for Memphis. He also told them that the man who piloted the plane and the hostage left in a car that appeared to have been left for them. Harris told them that he observed the hostage being tied and placed in the backseat. It appeared, according to Harris, that she was told to stay down and out of sight. That car was being followed by another agent and he was in radio contact with Harris. The other passenger in the plane, a younger man, left with the Watkins lady in her car. That car, too, was being tailed by an FBI agent and they, too, were in radio contact with Harris.

"Okay," said Bryan, "we want to get into contact with the agent who is following the man and woman. We need to know where they are and whether or not it looks like they are settling in for the night or driving on through."

Agent Harris had run a trace on any property nearby that might be connected to Billy Bowers or his construction company near Shreveport. He told Bryan and the others that the only property was a fishing cabin near Wallace Lake about twenty or thirty miles south of the city just off Interstate 49. They made the decision to send a squad there by helicopter about two hours ago, which was instructed to stay out of sight and let Agent Harris know if anyone showed up. Just as Bryan, Joe and Jan were about to drive away from the airport, they got a radio message from the squad at Wallace Lake telling them that two cars had driven to the cabin about thirty minutes apart. They described a man in the first car that matched the description of Dan Bowers, and the later car appeared to be Billy Bowers and Grace Watkins.

Chapter 35
Shreveport

After Dan had landed the plane, he took Kathy and ran to a waiting car that had been left there for him, while his son ran to a car that was parked just outside the fence driven by Grace. The instructions that Billy gave Dan were to drive south on I-49 out of town and to get off at the first exit to Wallace Lake. It would be marked Southern Loop. He was supposed to go east until he got to the Wallace Lake turnoff on the right and stay on the road until it dead ended. There were no distances on the instructions that were very precise so he would have to look out for them. Kathy was tied and gagged and put into the backseat, then bound in such a way that she could not sit up.

Billy and Grace were going to the same cabin but they were taking a longer route and with a few stops included, in case they were being followed or someone had followed Grace to the airport. Dan drove away from the airport and very easily found I-49 South, and entered the expressway cautiously. He took careful note of any cars that might be following him and there appeared to be none that stayed behind him very long so he continued at a safe speed until he got to the exit that was designated on his map. When the road dead ended at the lake, there were two gravel roads that formed a "Y" and he took the right fork. It was obvious that this road was rarely used, grass and weeds growing in the center which dragged along the bottom of the car. It was very dark and the fog was beginning to settle in on the lake, so Dan had to drive extra slow. After a few minutes, the road stopped at a clapboard house with a tin roof and a front porch across the front of the house that was partially falling down. He parked the car in the back so it would not be seen from the driveway and got Kathy from the back seat.

"Come on, Kathy," he ordered, as he pulled her out of the car. "Let's go inside and wait for Billy Boy to arrive."

She stumbled out of the car and followed him into the old cabin. The steps leading up to the porch were partly rotted so they walked gingerly up the steps and onto the front porch. Billy had told him that the key would be on top of the porch roof joist just above the door. He felt over the top of the timber and found the key and unlocked the front door. The cabin smelled musty and unused. Most of the furniture was covered with sheets and Dan began to yank them off and pile them in the center of the floor.

"Sit right here," he said to Kathy, pointing to an old rocker.

She sat in the rocker and Dan tied her arms to the armrests of the chair. After he was sure she was bound securely, he began to look around the house, opening each door and looking inside, making sure no one else was there. In a few minutes, he returned to the room and sat across from Kathy in a straight back chair. He moved the chair over closely to her and began to remove the gag from her mouth.

"Now, first of all let me warn you," he began, "there is no one around here within five miles, so screaming and hollering will do you no good. How this goes down is entirely up to you. But I planned on an hour alone with you, so let's make the most of it."

He untied her hands from the chair and helped her up and led her into the bedroom that was off to the right of the parlor where they were. Kathy had realized that sooner or later, this time was coming, and she had decided that it would be much better for her to cooperate with Dan and to let him have what he wanted because she knew he would take it from her otherwise.

"Now let's see what I've missed here for the last thirty years," said Dan as they sat on the edge of the bed and he began to remove her clothing.

He removed each piece of clothing slowly and kissed her nakedness beneath each piece. He then stood beside the bed and removed his own clothes and moved over close to her and sat on the edge of the bed beside her. He took one of her breasts and began to caress it gently with his fingers and placed the other hand between her thighs and into the warmness there. He pushed her back on the bed and moved over her as she laid back. She closed her eyes and tried to imagine being somewhere else with someone else but the fear was still there within her. He inserted his finger into her and she let out a small whimper from the pain. He continued to move his finger inside her until it was moist and then he entered her. Surprisingly to her, he was very gentle and he was trying very hard to not make it feel like the rape that it really was. She found herself fighting the nausea and unbearable pain and soon, he collapsed on top of her as he finished. She lay motionless under his weight and he finally moved off her and rolled to the side of her body.

Although Dan knew this was by no means what he had enjoyed with her years ago, it was, however, a victory for him personally. This represented vengeance for her rejection from years ago that he had carried deep within for so long. He had performed the ultimate act to ensure that they would be together forever, and she had rejected him.

"That wasn't so bad, was it?" he said as he looked back into her eyes. She was careful not to upset him, but had a very difficult time looking at him. When she did, all she could see was the murderer of her husband and God only knows how many other people. She thought of Jan and had no idea where she was or if she had survived her ordeal with the other man. She prayed that she wasn't going through the same humiliation that she was right now. She didn't know how she would ever get away from this man she so despised, but she knew that the possibility was there that she might be a prisoner forever.

"It's been a long time, Dan," she said, trying to sound as pleased as he seemed to want her to be.

"Well, sweet thing, we've got plenty of time to rekindle what we had once," he said with a sneer as he looked down on her while he stood by the bed naked. He appeared pleased with his conquest and Kathy was hopeful that Dan was indeed satisfied.

Dan reached down and picked up his Levis and sat on the edge of the bed and put them back on. He then reached down and picked up Kathy's clothing and threw them to her as she lay with the covers pulled over her body.

"Put these back on," he ordered her. "I've got to get you tied back up and wait on Billy and his girlfriend."

He sat there until she had put on her clothes and then took her by the arm and led her back into the front room and retied her to the chair. It was as if there were two men in the cabin with her, and Kathy feared them both. But she especially feared the man that Dan had become since he had finished having his way with her. He was more forceful and more demanding as he grabbed her and swung her through the door and pushed her onto the rocking chair once more. Kathy knew that she had to do whatever was necessary to stay on his good side for the time being.

She forced a smile as he looked at her and tried to show her acceptance of the situation. She was in no position to do anything else. After he tied her, he looked into her eyes and began to talk to her.

"I'd sure like some more of that, but I'm afraid we wouldn't have time so we'll save seconds for later on down the road."

"I'll be looking forward to it," Kathy said with as much enthusiasm as she could muster.

"I'm sure you will, you lying bitch," he said as he slapped her across the cheek with such force that her head snapped to the left.

Kathy decided that the best thing to do at the moment was to say as little as possible and to just sit it out and wait. There was always a possibility that help was on the way or a hope that she could later escape from Dan. She'd just have to be patient and wait it out.

After what seemed like thirty or forty minutes, headlights from an approaching car appeared in the front window. Dan looked out the blinds and saw that Billy had pulled into the drive with Grace and the money. He moved over to the door and removed the latch and greeted them on the front porch. Billy was carrying the case that contained the money and he handed it to his dad when he walked up the steps on the front porch.

"I haven't had a chance to count it all," he said, "but it looks like it's all there."

"There'll be plenty of time for counting later. Y'all come on in and let's talk," Dan said to them both.

They both entered the cabin and saw Kathy tied to the chair in the middle of the room. Grace became concerned about her being there and suggested that maybe it would be better for everyone if she was tied up in the bedroom out of sight. Dan let her know that she was going to stay right there and that is where she stayed.

"I'll take her in the bedroom with me in a few minutes and you guys can sleep out here on this old sleeper sofa. I'm planning on us getting out of here about four in the morning so we can get more miles behind us." Dan said it all in a matter-of-fact sort of way that left it obvious that there was no option.

"Okay, Pop," answered Billy. "Just wake us up and we'll get ready early."

Chapter 36
South of Shreveport

Joe sat in the front seat of Harris's car as they drove out of the airport and headed the same route that Dan Bowers had taken about an hour earlier. Bryan and Jan sat in the back seat, and Bryan took hold of her hand in an attempt to calm her down and to reassure her. He turned to her and looked her in the eyes as he talked.

"We've got three cars there with agents and they have stayed out of sight," he told her. "They've got everything pretty well staked out and we'll get in there quietly and hopefully take them by surprise."

Just as he finished, the radio in the car came to life. An agent on the scene was reporting in on the activity there.

"Agent Wilson checking in from the scene," the radio said.

"Go ahead Wilson, this is Harris," he answered. "We're leaving the airport and are about twenty minutes out. What's the situation there?"

"The second car came in about ten minutes ago and a man and woman entered the cabin. Looked like the guy was carrying a rifle across his shoulder and the lady was carrying a couple of bags," Wilson answered.

Joe commented to Harris that by the time they got there, the four people inside the cabin should be settled in. He and Bryan both agreed

255

that it would be best to stay out of sight as long as possible and try to catch them after they had settled in for the night. They all agreed that there would probably be someone awake to stand guard and that the likelihood of a complete surprise was not very good. With only one person to get through, there was hope that this could be done quickly with a minimum of gunfire that might endanger Kathy.

"Where would be the best place to meet you guys without alerting the four inside the cabin?" Harris asked Wilson.

"As you come in toward the lake, there is a fork in the road where it appears to dead end," instructed Wilson. "That spot is about a half mile back from the cabin and out of sight. We'll walk back there and meet you."

"That sounds good," said Harris. "We'll be there by the time you walk back. Are you leaving someone there to watch for activity?"

"I'm planning on leaving three of the guys here and taking a couple with me. See you in about ten minutes."

He signed off, and Joe turned to Bryan and Jan in the back seat.

"Looks like all this is finally going to come to an end," he said to them. "I'm sure this guy is confident that he was not followed here and that there will be no problem for a while."

"That's the one thing that we have in our favor," agreed Bryan. "Hopefully we can get in and get your mother out of there safely." He squeezed her hand to reassure her.

As they pulled onto the dead end of the road and to the forks where the meeting was to take place, Harris cut off his engine and lights and sat quietly until Wilson and the other agents appeared just in front of them. He instructed Joe and Bryan to exit the car and not to make any noises as they met the three agents who had been staking out the site. Harris ordered Jan to stay in the car, and after Bryan's reassuring nod, she agreed.

"We've been here about three hours now," began Wilson. "After we arrived we walked around the property to see about escape routes from the cabin."

"What've we got here?" asked Bryan.

"Well," answered Wilson, "this road here is the only way in or out of here. They can go out by boat. There's a boat in the boat house behind the house, but it doesn't look like it's been used in a while. Not likely they'll try that route."

"What about cover behind the house if they come out that way?" asked Bryan.

"The back yard is very steep and there are steps leading down to the lake from the cabin," answered Wilson.

"So what is the situation now if we try to go in there?" asked Joe.

"I'm pretty sure," answered Wilson, "that the hostage is being kept in the back bedroom and there is not much room in the front of the house. As far as weapons, we have very little knowledge of that. It's possible that weapons could have been stored there before they arrived."

"I agree," said Bryan. "There are too many unknowns to go storming in there and attempting a rescue. Too many things could go wrong."

"Look," said Joe, "this place right here is the best place I've seen to attempt a rescue. This is the only way out and they have to be going slow up that dirt road and into the fork right here."

Harris agreed with Joe's idea of how the seizure should take place.

"So we've got this in our favor," said Bryan. "They have no idea that we are here; I think they feel safe for the night. It's the element of surprise that we have in our favor. Let's set it up right here and hit them quickly."

Wilson called the men who were watching the cabin and instructed one of them to stay and watch the cabin and the other two to move quietly to the fork in the road. They were instructed not to turn on flashlights or make noise, and to take their time. Harris told them they had plenty of time and that they did not want to alert them of their presence.

Billy had taken the first shift as guard and stood up from his chair on the front porch and began walking across the front of the house. The lone agent was hidden about fifty yards on the opposite side of the road from the cabin and watching with binoculars as best he could. When Billy moved to the right side of the cabin, he lost sight of him and did not know where he was for ten or fifteen minutes until he reappeared on the left side of the cabin walking back toward the front porch. He shone his flashlight into the woods all around the cabin, then walked back up the steps and into the rocker he had been sitting in. As he sat back down and lit a cigarette, a raccoon scuttled along the ground between himself and the agent who was watching some distance to his left. He jumped from the chair and moved with his flashlight to investigate, with his pistol straight out in front of him. As he walked into the woods, the raccoon ran along the trail in front of him creating a loud crunching of leaves and brush and causing Billy to fire a couple of shots into the direction he was running.

At the sound of the shots, the agent moved deeper into the brush to hide from the approaching light. Also at the sound of the shots, Dan came running out the front door of the cabin with his rifle to his shoulder and a flashlight wobbling in the shooting hand. He moved off the steps and over into the wooded area where Billy was now shining his light frantically into the woods. The raccoon had moved over to his right and had managed to scurry up a tree and was watching the confusion from high above in a live oak tree. Dan ran down to where Billy was standing.

"I think I saw someone down here," said Billy anxiously as he continued to shine his light into the woods.

"Did you see someone, or did you hear a noise?" asked Dan.

"I saw some movement down this way and heard a noise over this way," he answered, pointing over into the woods in the direction the raccoon had run.

Dan walked deeper into the woods and was shining his light into the trees when the eyes of the terrified raccoon came into view.

"There's your noise, Billy," he said loudly, and Billy ran into the woods to see his dad pointing into the tree with his light in the eyes of the intruder.

"It's a raccoon, and I'm sure there are a lot of them out here," Dan explained. "Hasn't been anyone out here in a long time, and they're used to having the run of the place. Why don't you go in a catch some shut-eye, I'll watch for a couple of hours and then we'll switch again."

"Okay, Pop," Billy answered. "Sorry about that."

"That's okay, boy, just be out in a couple of hours so I can catch a snooze or two before we hit the road."

Billy moved back into the house, and Dan took his place in the rocker on the front porch. He laid his rifle across his lap, lit a cigarette and started rocking. After the shots, the agents at the fork in the road had joined the other agent who was watching the house and motioned him over to point just over the hill where they could not be heard.

"What happened?" asked Harris.

"Oh, the younger guy got a little trigger happy and fired into the woods at a raccoon," the agent replied. "I'm just glad I was in the opposite direction."

"This would be great time to hit them," chimed in Bryan. "They've just changed positions and I would bet that Kathy is alone in the back room, with the other two in the front room."

"Might be a good time to change plans," suggested Harris.

Bryan pointed around the house and began to explain his plan to them.

"Give me about fifteen minutes," he began. "I'm going to work my way around the back of the house and after I get into position, draw their attention and make them fire toward you. I'll see if I can go in the back and grab Kathy out of there and then we can take them with her safe."

"Sounds like good plan to me. We'll draw their fire in fifteen minutes from right now," Harris said looking at his watch.

"All right," said Bryan checking his watch, "I'm gone." He ran quickly and quietly to the right and began working his way around the back of the house.

Dan sat on the front porch with a cigar and puffed on it while he looked out at the woods. The rocker made a squeaking noise with the weathered loose boards it sat on. It helped to hide any noise that Bryan might make as he walked quietly through the woods.

It took Bryan eleven minutes to work his way around the house and get into position at the steps in the back. There was a small stoop there, where the back door opened and Bryan worked his way under the rail onto that stoop where he sat and waited for the next four minutes to tick away.

Right on cue, Harris and his men began move to the left, closer to the cabin but out of the line of fire. When they got close enough, they began to make intentional noise which brought Dan out of the rocker and down the front steps. Harris fired a shot in the direction of Dan and instantly, Billy came charging out the front door. As Billy crashed out the front door, Bryan crashed through the back door and ran into the bedroom where Kathy was tied to a chair. With his knife, he cut the ropes and scooped her in his arms and ran back out the back door before anyone knew he was there. He told her to lie flat on the ground behind a bush until he was sure it was safe to run to the boat house below. When Dan and Billy began to fire at the agents, Bryan and Kathy went scurrying down the steep steps to the boat house and went inside.

Dan and Billy decided that the best thing to do was to work their way back to the cabin and they went back through the front door and smashed the front windows so they could shoot at anyone approaching. Grace had awakened from the couch where she was sleeping and Billy handed her a handgun and told her to go and check on Kathy. She returned seconds later with the news that Kathy had escaped.

"All that noise must have been a diversion to draw our attention," said Dan as he looked out the broken glass.

During the confusion a couple of the agents had managed to work their way around the back of the house and were guarding the back door, just in case they attempted to come out that way. After everyone was in position, Harris tried to communicate with the three inside the house.

Joe handed the bullhorn to Agent Harris and he barked out his ultimatum.

"Look, Dan," he yelled. "There is no way out of there. We've already got your hostage out of there, and we've got you completely surrounded."

To this ultimatum, Dan began to fire rapid shots in succession in the direction of the voice. After the shooting stopped, Joe tossed a grenade of tear gas through the other window and the house began to fill rapidly with a thick fog.

Dan, Billy, and Grace began to make their way to the back door just as another canister came through the kitchen window in front of them, blocking their escape out the back. Grace ran out the front door with her hands in the air and was quickly brought under control by one of the agents and handcuffed. In a matter of seconds, Billy came out coughing with his hands in the air. He, too, was captured and cuffed and placed under the control of another of the agents. After a span of two minutes, a gunshot rang out from inside the house, and everyone knew that Dan had decided to end it himself.

The agents stormed into the house and found Dan lying in a pool of blood at the foot of the bed. He had shot himself with one of his pistols under the chin as blood and brain matter cluttered the nearby wall.

When the shooting started, Bryan and Kathy had made their way back up the steps, through the woods and back to the waiting FBI cars, where Jan had been waiting frantically for them to return. When the gunfire began, she had stepped outside the car and was still standing there, searching the woods, when Bryan and her mother appeared in the clearing of the road. She ran to her mother and hugged her, tears in her eyes. She then turned her attention to Bryan and hugged him and thanked him for returning her mother safely.

"You've got a good man there, Jan," her mom said to her as she and Bryan embraced. "I wouldn't let him get away if I were you."

"I don't plan to, Mom," she said as he looked into Bryan's eyes and they kissed.

As they looked around, they noticed that a full moon had risen and appeared through the clouds and a deep purple haze was settling just over the lake ahead.

Purple Haze

Epilogue
Nashville, 1972

Kathy and Frank were very excited as they sat on their patio behind their house in Nashville. Jan was arriving at any moment with her husband Bryan and their grandson, Jimi. He had been named after Jimi Hendrix as a memorial to that first weekend they spent together and the rock festival in Georgia that marked their first date. Jan and Bryan married shortly after the kidnapping and were living in Chattanooga where Bryan worked as a division supervisor for the FBI and Jan worked as a feature writer and reporter for the *Chattanooga News Free Press*.

"It's been almost three months since we've seen them," Frank said as he took hold of her hand.

"Yeah," agreed Kathy. "They've been pretty busy with their work."

Since the shootout in Louisiana, Billy had gone to trial for conspiracy and racketeering, and had been convicted of killing a couple of the men at the Rome airport. He had been given consecutive life sentences and would never see freedom again. His girlfriend, Grace, had turned State's evidence and her testimony helped to bring down several of the people involved in Billy's construction company and its ties to racketeering.

Kathy had a difficult time putting all the terrible events of that week behind her, but she had managed to do so, and her husband Frank had been a great help to her in her recovery. Since the birth of their grandson, she had made frequent trips to Chattanooga and had tried to stay in touch as much as possible. Her life had once again become a happy one, and the things that happened to her were left in the past and she looked forward to the future.

They heard a car pull up in the driveway. They arose and ran through the gate to the front yard. Little Jimi ran excitedly to his grandmother and jumped up in her arms when she reached out for him. Jan walked over to her dad and hugged him enthusiastically, and Bryan shook his hand. They all walked into the house together, and no mention was made of the events that brought them all together for the first time. There was only talk of the present and the future. And that seemed to be a bright one indeed.

About the Author

George Hudson was born in East Tennessee in 1947, into a family of seven other siblings. His life was deeply impacted by the Tennessee Valley Authority and by the lakes throughout the area in which he was raised. He has been a lifetime educator, teaching history in the public schools in Tennessee for thirty years. George also taught as an adjunct professor of history and is presently teaching at the University of Tennessee-Chattanooga. In his writing, he intersperses bits of history about the area to add local color and sentiment. He and his wife, Gail, live in Chattanooga.

Purple Haze

If you enjoyed *Purple Haze,* consider these other fine books from
Savant Books and Publications:

Essay, Essay, Essay by Yasuo Kobachi
Aloha from Coffee Island by Walter Miyanari
Footprints, Smiles and Little White Lies by Daniel S. Janik
The Illustrated Middle Earth by Daniel S. Janik
Last and Final Harvest by Daniel S. Janik
A Whale's Tale by Daniel S. Janik
Tropic of California by R. Page Kaufman
Tropic of California (the companion music CD) by R. Page Kaufman
The Village Curtain by Tony Tame
Dare to Love in Oz by William Maltese
The Interzone by Tatsuyuki Kobayashi
Today I Am a Man by Larry Rodness
The Bahrain Conspiracy by Bentley Gates
Called Home by Gloria Schumann
Kanaka Blues by Mike Farris
First Breath edited by Z. M. Oliver
Poor Rich by Jean Blasiar
The Jumper Chronicles by W. C. Peever
William Maltese's Flicker by William Maltese
My Unborn Child by Orest Stocco
Last Song of the Whales by Four Arrows
Perilous Panacea by Ronald Klueh
Falling but Fulfilled by Zachary M. Oliver
Mythical Voyage by Robin Ymer
Hello, Norma Jean by Sue Dolleris
Richer by Jean Blasiar
Manifest Intent by Mike Farris
Charlie No Face by David B. Seaburn
Number One Bestseller by Brian Morley
My Two Wives and Three Husbands by S. Stanley Gordon
In Dire Straits by Jim Currie
Wretched Land by Mila Komarnisky
Chan Kim by Ilan Herman

Who's Killing All the Lawyers? by A. G. Hayes
Ammon's Horn by G. Amati
Wavelengths edited by Zachary M. Oliver
Almost Paradise by Laurie Hanan
Communion by Jean Blasiar and Jonathan Marcantoni
The Oil Man by Leon Puissegur
Random Views of Asia from the Mid-Pacific by William E. Sharp
The Isla Vista Crucible by Reilly Ridgell
Blood Money by Scott Mastro
In the Himalayan Nights by Anoop Chandola
On My Behalf by Helen Doan
Traveler's Rest by Jonathan Marcantoni
Keys in the River by Tendai Mwanaka
Chimney Bluffs by David B. Seaburn
The Loons by Sue Dolleris
Light Surfer by David Allan Williams
The Judas List by A. G. Hayes
Path of the Templar - Book 2 of The Jumper Chronicles by W. C. Peever
Shutterbug by Buz Sawyer
The Desperate Cycle by Tony Tame
Blessed are the Peacekeepers by Tim Donnelly and Mike Munger
Bellwether Messages edited by Daniel S. Janik

Soon To be Released:
The Lazarus Conspiracies by Richard Rose
The Hanging of Dr. Hanson by Bentley Gates
Imminent Danger by A. G. Hayes

www.savantbooksandpublications.com

www.ingramcontent.com/pod-product-compliance
Lightning Source LLC
Chambersburg PA
CBHW071130260626
47162CB00003B/733